THE LAST
MERIAH

Some roots don't thicken. They deepen.

JITU MISHRA

VIDYA PUBLISHING INC.

The Last Meriah

Jitu Mishra

Vidya Publishing Inc.

The Last Meriah
Author: Jitu Mishra

....

ISBN: 978-1-99847-596-4 52499

First Edition:	August, 2025
Published by:	**Dr. Tanmay Panda &**
	Dr. Sunanda Mishra Panda
	Vidya Publishing Inc.,
	Toronto, Canada || Bhubaneswar, India
Website:	**www.vidyapublishing.com**
Email:	vidyapublishinginc@gmail.com
Cell:	+1 6478389884
India Contact:	Nirmalya Garden, Plot 516/1719, House 10,
	KIIT Post Office, Bhubaneswar - 751024
Cell:	+91 8984131810
Cover Design:	**Jitu Mishra**
	Printed in India, Biswanath Enterprises

Price: ` 499 /-

The P N Choudhury Foundation is a non-profit trust dedicated to empowering communities through education, cultural preservation, and sustainable development. Founded to create lasting social impact in Odisha and beyond, it supports educational initiatives, health programs, and environmental stewardship.

Key beliefs include:

1. Knowledge, compassion, and cultural continuity as pillars of a resilient society.
2. Ensuring progress does not compromise cultural identity.

Led by Shri Prashant Choudhury, Dr. Mousumi Dash, Smt. Padmavati Choudhury, and Urmi Choudhury, in memory of Late Shri Narasingha Choudhury, the Foundation focuses on:

1. Education for All: Access to quality learning for underserved communities.
2. Cultural Preservation: Protecting Odisha's rich heritage.
3. Sustainable Development: Promoting ecological balance in livelihoods.

In collaboration with The Last Meriah, the Foundation amplifies indigenous voices and shares impactful stories, fostering dialogue and cultural pride. It is committed to preserving memory, identity, and the spirit of the land and its people.

AUTHOR'S NOTE

Jitu Mishra

This book began not as a plot, but as a pulse — a quiet hum I felt while walking through the forests of Odisha many years ago. I was not looking for a story then. I was simply listening.

I had heard of the Meriah ritual through colonial records, anthropological texts, and missionary accounts — most of which framed it with fear, revulsion, or moral conquest. But as I wandered deeper into the oral landscapes of Kandhamal, what I found was not a story of savagery, but of sorrow. Not brutality, but memory. Not a ritual of sacrifice, but a ceremony of renewal that had been misunderstood, interrupted, and mourned.

The Kondh people, with their spiritual relationship to the forest, taught me that resistance does not always roar. Sometimes it sings, sometimes it spirals — drawn in turmeric and ash, walked barefoot in silence, passed down in breath.

What moved me most was the way the Kondh community transformed Meriah — turning what was once a ritual involving blood into a nonviolent invocation of memory. I began to imagine a woman — Eliza — who came from the colonial world but did not try to "fix" or "study" what she saw. Instead, she listened. And then Thomas, who stood between survey maps and sacred roots. And Shami, Amma, Biruka — characters shaped by the people, landscapes, and quiet wisdoms I have witnessed through years of walking, researching, and feeling deeply with this land.

Eliza

A British ethnographer in a Kondh village

Jitu Mishra

THOMAS

A curious artist, learning to see
with his heart

But it didn't end there.

As I worked through the pages, I realized that the spiral was still unfolding — across time. The question arose: What happens when such a memory is rediscovered in a world grappling with climate collapse, food insecurity, and cultural amnesia? That is when Sophie emerged — the great-great-granddaughter, carrying not just a genetic legacy, but the spiritual aftershock of an interrupted grove.

This novel is my tribute to the Kondh community, and to indigenous peoples across the world who have long been seen as peripheral — when in truth, their wisdom lies at the very center of survival. It is a call to listen — not with pity or romanticism, but with humility. It is an invitation to rethink how we remember, what we value, and how we move forward without uprooting what still nourishes us.

I remain deeply indebted to those who shared fragments, songs, silences, and memories. And to the forests — who never speak loudly, but who always remember.

Thank you for walking the spiral with me.

— Jitu Mishra

Dedication

To the women of Mundigada, Baliguda, Belghar, Desughati,
and the many quiet villages of Kandhamal,
where sal trees whisper stories that maps and records
forgot.

To the elders who guarded memory in their silence,
and to the children who drew spirals in dust,
as if answering a call older than language.

To the forest paths, the turmeric groves, and the breath of
fog at dawn
that taught me listening is deeper than knowing.

And to my mother,
whose quiet strength mirrored the hills —
rooted, fierce, and full of forgotten songs.

The Last Meriah

Chapter 1
Whispers from Oxford

The Last Meriah

Oxford, 1875

Fog floated over Radcliffe Square like breath from the dreaming past, curling around the buttresses of stone colleges, weaving between gaslamps, cloisters, and horse-hooves on slick cobbles. The rain had stopped just an hour ago, but the world still glistened—wet slate roofs, dripping ivy, and puddles that mirrored towers too ancient to crumble.

Inside the echoing chambers of All Souls College, the silence was older than memory. Shadows lingered like scholars in long coats. Oil portraits stared from walls darkened by time and coal soot, their painted eyes unblinking.

In a corner of the library's long gallery, Eliza Ashford bent over a book bound in green leather and faded gold. Her brow furrowed, not from confusion, but from a kind of hunger. She was twenty-four—too old to be a student, too young to be dismissed, and too brilliant to be ignored for much longer.

She shouldn't have been there. Oxford in 1875 didn't formally accept women. But Eliza had entered through side doors—through mentorships, footnotes, and sheer intellectual gravity. Her father, a liberal Member of Parliament, disapproved but funded her curiosity in silence. It was her uncle, a retired East India Company officer turned orientalist, who had sparked her early fascination with tribal myths and rituals from the lands beyond the Raj.

Now she was a quiet storm in the margins of academia—reading Sanskrit in whispered corners, attending lectures from behind curtains, and corresponding with ethnographers across the empire under initials alone.

The Last Meriah

The book in her hands was dense, its script hand-copied from missionary records. One passage caught her breath:

"...The Kondh tribes of the Ganjam Agency hold the Earth to be a goddess, Dharani Penu. To her, they offer a girl—called the Meriah—nurtured for years, anointed, venerated, and finally returned to the soil through ritual sacrifice, in the belief that her blood renews the fertility of the land."

She paused. Not from horror.

From recognition.

This was not murder. Not to them. This was offering. Faith, in its rawest and most misunderstood form.

She lifted her head.

Across the table, Thomas Elliot, her closest companion in work—and perhaps, in ways neither of them dared admit, in life—was sketching a curved dagger, copied from a monograph on South Indian tribal weapons. He was tall, quiet, precise in everything. The son of a former Company surveyor who had died in Assam during a border expedition, Thomas had grown up between cultures. His father's notebooks and half-finished maps had become his childhood toys.

He never said much, but he understood silence better than most.

"Eliza?" he said softly, looking up.

She turned the book toward him. "They believed she was the Earth herself. Raised in kindness, fed with turmeric and ghee, adorned with bangles. Then, one day... offered back."

The Last Meriah

He blinked. "To renew the land."

She nodded.

"They called it a sacrifice. But it was more than that."

Before he could reply, a knock echoed through the tall arched doorway.

A messenger entered—a young porter in damp boots, clutching a folded coat in one hand and a cream-coloured envelope in the other. It bore the unmistakable red wax seal of the British India Office.

To Miss Eliza Ashford and Mr. Thomas Elliot
All Souls College, Oxford

By recommendation of the Royal Asiatic Society and in light of your recent contributions to the study of comparative ritual systems, you are invited to undertake a scholarly expedition to the tribal highlands of Ganjam and Kandhamal, Madras Presidency. The purpose: to observe and document the belief systems, sacred practices, and social organization of the Kondh communities. The mission has been approved under the oversight of the India Office. Passage on the P&O steamer S.S. Madura to Calcutta is scheduled for 14 days from today. Travel provisions and honorarium will be arranged. Further instruction to follow.

Thomas exhaled slowly. He read the letter again. Eliza was already standing, the letter in one hand, her journal in the other.

"You've been waiting for this," he said.

"I've been preparing for it," she replied.

"You know the risks," he said. "The hills are not just geography. They're rebellion, resistance. There have been uprisings. Hostility."

Eliza's eyes held a quiet fire.

"Then it's time someone arrived not with guns," she said, "but with ears."

Outside, the bell at All Souls tolled six times. The sky beyond the windows turned the colour of wet iron. The fog was rising again, wrapping Oxford in its gentle grip.

Somewhere beyond the seas, on a slope between turmeric fields and sacred groves, a girl waited to be remembered.

And Eliza was ready to begin.

Chapter 2
The Journey Eastward

The Last Meriah

Calcutta, August 1875

The S.S. Madura docked at the Kidderpore Port just before dawn, the ship's long whistle dissolving into the humid air like a hymn. Eliza stood at the rail, fingers curled around the damp brass, watching as the banks of the Hooghly emerged from the grey. Palms stood like guardians. Wooden boats clattered against one another. The city was not yet awake—but it breathed.

Behind her, Thomas closed his sketchbook. It was the fifth he had filled since they left England.

Calcutta overwhelmed the senses. It smelled of turmeric, molasses, ash, jasmine, and river mud. Bullocks pulled carts beside horse-drawn carriages. Stray dogs howled in alleys. And above the din rose cupolas and clock towers —British ambition carved in stone, pressed against a sky that always seemed too wide.

They stayed two days in a Government guesthouse near Fort William, close to the river. A senior officer from the India Office met them there, brief and clipped.

"You'll find the hills resistant, especially the Kondhs. They are not like the plainsmen. You must not wander far without escort. And you are to report monthly—any mention of the Meriah must be documented with precision. Understood?"

Eliza had nodded, though the man had barely addressed her. Thomas simply noted the name of their civil liaison: Mr. Caldwell, posted in Ganjam.

The Last Meriah

Their journey to the interior began with the East Indian Railway, departing from Howrah station. The train hissed and rumbled its way southwest, past rice paddies, lotus-covered ponds, and villages crowned with mango groves. Women washed saris in streams. Temple bells tolled faintly in the morning air. Crows followed the train like omens.

By the second day, they reached Cuttack, the end of the railway's reach in this region. The tracks had not yet extended to Ganjam, and certainly not into Kandhamal.

From here, the journey turned backward in time.

A convoy awaited them—three bullock carts for supplies, a palanquin for Eliza (though she refused it), and a group of porters hired from the lower plains. They were to travel southward through narrow forest paths, riverbeds, and tribal hamlets toward Berhampur, and beyond it, the Kondh highlands.

The pace was slow, the monsoon had not fully withdrawn, and the roads were little more than wet clay.

On the fourth day, as they crossed a bamboo footbridge over a swollen stream, a tribal youth appeared on the trail ahead. Bare-chested, with skin the colour of polished teak, and eyes like obsidian. He carried no weapon, only a cloth satchel and a turmeric-stained thread around his neck.

Their guide approached him. Words in Kui were exchanged. Then the youth nodded and pointed westward—into the hills.

The Last Meriah

"That," the guide whispered to Thomas, "is Biruka. He has been sent ahead by the village elders. They know you are coming."

That night, they camped near a clearing lit by fireflies. Eliza wrote in her journal by lamplight:

"We are no longer in Bengal. The sounds are different. The air is thicker. There are no churches. No spires. Only trees, rising like chants into the sky. I feel as though we are entering not just land—but memory."

Thomas said little. He drew the silhouette of a Kondh axe carved into a tree nearby—its handle wrapped in red thread.

He did not know what the symbol meant.

But he felt it watched them.

They would reach the edge of Ganjam in two more days. From there, they would ascend into the sacred hills— where the Earth had a name, and blood had once been its language.

Neither of them spoke it yet.

But they would learn.

Chapter 3
At the Edge of Empire

Jitu Mishra

Near Ganjam, August 1875

The colonial resthouse was nothing like the quiet order of Fort William. It leaned slightly to one side, as if the forest had been trying for years to reclaim it. Vines crept up the stone veranda, geckos scattered under the wooden floorboards, and the bell that hung by the entrance had rusted into silence.

Eliza stepped out of the bullock cart, her boots sinking slightly into damp earth. The air was thicker here—green, alive, and pulsing with insect-song. The trail behind them had narrowed for miles until it was barely wide enough for a cart. Now it ended here, before a low-slung bungalow with a red tin roof and a Union Jack that barely stirred.

A lean man in a creased cotton uniform greeted them on the steps.

"Mr. Caldwell," he introduced himself, offering a hand first to Thomas. "District Assistant, Ganjam Agency. You'll find the forest does not care for titles, but we try anyway."

Thomas nodded. Eliza gave a polite bow. Caldwell's eyes lingered on her, puzzled but not unkind.

"You'll want to rest before heading into the uplands. It's not a journey best made with sharp minds dulled."

The bungalow had three rooms and an open dining porch shaded by a frayed canvas awning. A single Kondh boy swept the yard with a short broom, moving silently between the shadows of the jackfruit trees. Eliza noticed he had a scar across his forearm—not from accident, but clean, ceremonial. She made a note in her journal.

Jitu Mishra

They were offered tea in enamel cups. The biscuits were damp with the weather.

At dinner, another officer joined them—Lt. Merriweather, posted there to oversee the surveying of new forest trails. He was younger, louder, and not particularly fond of the tribes.

"They say the hills speak," he chuckled, swirling his whisky. "But they're always lying. Half of them worship trees, the other half sacrifice children. Welcome to the edge of reason."

Eliza said nothing. Thomas shifted in his seat.

"A girl disappeared last week," Caldwell added flatly. "North of Belghar. Possibly Meriah."
"Not our concern. Yet," Merriweather replied, lighting a cigar.
"It might be," Eliza said softly, her voice calm but piercing. "If the girl believes she's meant to die, we should understand why."

The table fell quiet. A moth fluttered against the lamp glass.

That night, they slept under mosquito nets, but the sounds outside were louder than any net could contain.

Eliza heard drums—faint, pulsing, like a heartbeat deep within the hills.

She dreamed of turmeric fields under moonlight, of a girl standing barefoot before a pit, her body painted in yellow and red. No one pushed her. She walked in willingly.

Jitu Mishra

Thomas sat up late, sketching. In the margins of his map, he drew the shape of a tree—but its branches ended in blades.

At dawn, a message arrived on foot.

Biruka would meet them at the stone marker beyond the river crossing, where the jungle path truly began. He would take them the rest of the way.

A porter who had traveled with them from Cuttack refused to go further.

"It's Meriah season," he muttered. "The forest remembers blood."

Eliza stood quietly by the banyan, her hand resting on her journal.

Beyond the mist that clung to the treetops, the highlands waited—green, patient, and old.

They would not walk into maps now. They would walk into memory.

Chapter 4
The Forest and the Thread

The Last Meriah

The forest began where the road forgot its name.

Past the final bend of brittle gravel, the worn path gave way to mud, root, and leaf. Sunlight fractured through tall sal trees like scattered prayers. As the bullock cart groaned one last time behind them, Thomas and Eliza stood still. Biruka waited just ahead, barefoot and composed, as if the forest itself had asked him to guard its breath.

He did not speak.

Instead, he gestured to a stone marker—a weathered slab set beside a tree wrapped in strips of turmeric cloth and red thread, fluttering faintly in the morning air. A few cowry shells lay at its base beside a feather and a smear of blood turned rust.

"What does it mean?" Eliza asked softly.

Biruka looked toward the tree, not at her. "This is the knot between us and the Mother. We tie it so we do not forget."

Eliza stepped closer, fingers brushing the cloth. The thread trembled under her touch—not from wind, but perhaps memory.

They moved deeper in. Shoes came off. The earth was warm, yielding beneath their soles—damp from the previous night's rain and rich with decay. Birds called in layered harmony above, and somewhere, the cough of a distant animal broke the rhythm.

The Last Meriah

Biruka paused at a stream and smeared ash and crushed leaves on a stone. He whispered a prayer to Dharani Penu, goddess of the Earth, speaking in a voice both reverent and unafraid.

"This is not your land," he said. "But you came with your eyes open. The Mother has seen."

Eliza knelt beside him. "And if she disapproves?"

"Then the forest will tell us."

They walked in silence, passing ferns taller than a man, jackfruit trees draped with moss, and termite mounds shaped like forgotten gods. Eliza noted the scars on bark —symbols carved with blades, matching those she had seen in her books. Some resembled fish, others the eye of a spirit.

Thomas pointed to a tree.

"See this?" he said, sketching quickly. "A totem tattoo. It's the same as the one I saw in that Burmese ritual drawing."

Biruka glanced at the page. "Ours are not from Burma. They were given to us before there was language."

Near noon, the path opened onto a charred clearing. Smoke still drifted from ash pits and the scorched stumps of sal trees.

"Podu chasa," Biruka murmured. "Fire makes the land clean."

The Last Meriah

Eliza watched as two women in the distance sowed seeds into the blackened soil with long sticks, their faces smeared with turmeric and ash. Neither looked up.

Thomas sketched silently. Eliza wrote:

"Ritual, ecology, and memory—bound in flame."

By late afternoon, they reached a hillock overlooking a Kondh hamlet. Bamboo huts, thatched roofs, and the smell of millet brewing in clay pots. Smoke twisted into the golden air. Children's laughter mixed with the low thump of distant evening drums.

Biruka turned.

"You are not strangers now," he said, eyes resting briefly on Eliza. "But you are not yet known."

He stepped forward into the village.

Thomas adjusted his satchel. Eliza, barefoot and dusty, clutched her journal close.

"I feel like we've crossed something," she said.

"Not a line," Thomas replied. "A thread."

And they followed—into the rhythm of a people, into a place that held both beauty and blood.

Chapter 5
The Girl with the Drum-Tattoo

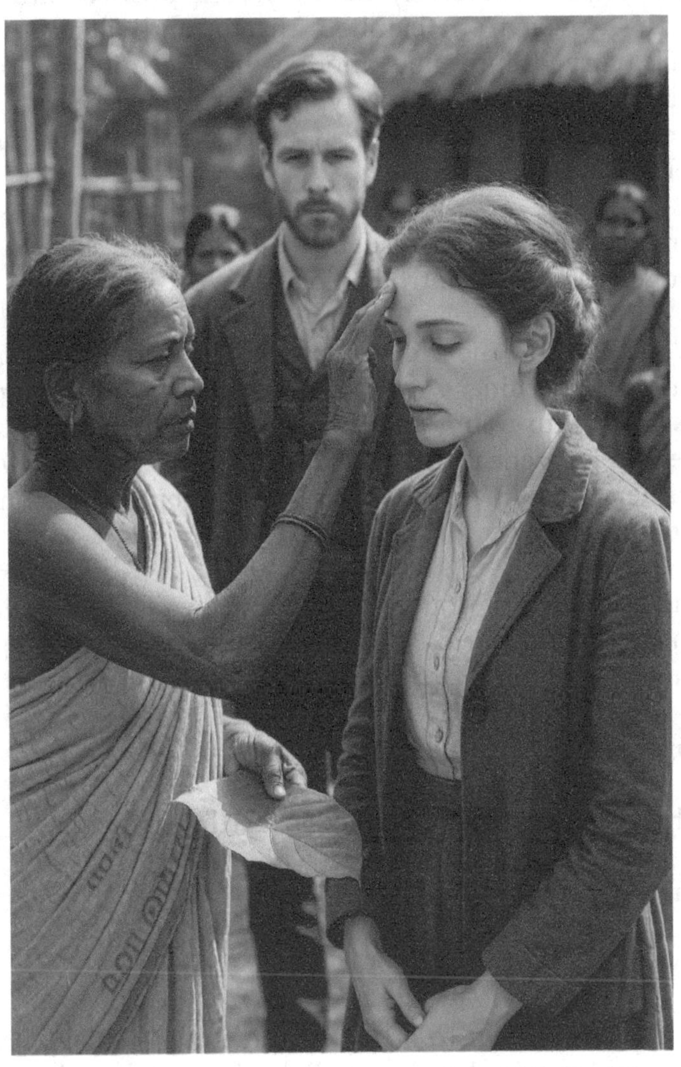

Jitu Mishra

They entered the village not as guests, but as questions.

The Kondh hamlet lay like a breath pressed into the earth—woven from bamboo, thatch, and silence. Mud walls curved into one another like termite mounds, spiraled with chalk-white glyphs. Smoke curled from low fires. Chickens darted across narrow paths. The forest held its breath.

Biruka walked ahead—silent, confident. He carried no badge, no token of introduction. He was the token.

At the edge of the village, a group of women watched. They said nothing. One woman stepped forward, dipped a sal leaf into water, and sprinkled it in an arc at Eliza's feet. Her forehead bore a white smear. Her eyes were neither hostile nor warm—just deeply, startlingly present.

Another woman touched Eliza's brow with a thumb smeared in turmeric and ash. She muttered something in Kui.

Eliza glanced at Biruka.

"She says... 'No blade in hand. So, earth permits.'"

Thomas gave a slight bow.

No one responded.

They were shown to a hut on the fringe—small, clean, rectangular, with bamboo walls and a thatched dome. A rolled mat, two clay pots, a folded cotton sheet. It was not hospitality—it was containment. But it was shelter.

Jitu Mishra

And it was a beginning.

That afternoon, while Thomas sketched rooflines and grain baskets, Eliza wandered toward the communal grinding stones. A circle of women sat under a neem tree, rhythmically crushing turmeric roots with flat stone grinders. Their hands were yellow. Their feet cracked with years of barefoot earth.

Eliza crouched beside them. Her attempt to sit cross-legged drew muffled laughter. She smiled, picked up a root, and began mimicking their motions.

One woman pointed to the paste and said something.

Eliza looked to Biruka, who stood a little behind.

"She say—'Haldi makes skin gold. Good for bride. Good for land.'"

Eliza nodded. "Teach me. How do you say it?"

Biruka hesitated.

She repeated: "Teach. Me."

He crouched beside her, slowly said, "Dharani dal gunu... sigin."

Eliza shaped the words in her mouth, awkward but eager.

The women giggled again, one patting her shoulder.

"She say... you sound like goat," Biruka smirked.

Eliza laughed, genuinely. "Then let the goat learn."

Jitu Mishra

But her attention drifted.

A girl—no older than thirteen—sat apart beneath a jackfruit tree. Her skin was dusted with turmeric. Her cheek and upper arm were marked with inked spirals— dark, deliberate, ceremonial.

She held a small hand drum and tapped it softly—no rhythm, just a searching beat.

None of the other women approached her.

"Who is she?" Eliza asked.

Biruka's smile faded. "She is... dohka. Marked."

"For what?"

He didn't answer.

That night, as firelight shimmered in courtyards and dogs barked at shadows, Thomas returned with sketches of forest paths and tattoo patterns. He sat beside Eliza near their hut, listening to the distant hum of drums rising from somewhere unseen.

"She's more than a girl," Eliza whispered. "Her tattoos... they match the Meriah carving we saw. The girl by the tree... she's not just marked. She's chosen."

Thomas looked uneasy. "We don't know that yet."

Eliza said nothing. Her fingers traced the spiral she had drawn in her journal.

"If she is the Meriah," she said softly, "then time is not on our side."

That night, in dreams, Eliza heard the drum.

It wasn't the girl who played it.

It was the earth.

Chapter 6
The Songs of Dharani Penu

Jitu Mishra

The rains had passed, but the earth still sighed beneath the trees.

Eliza stepped barefoot along a narrow, leaf-strewn path behind Biruka. The village had quieted after the morning turmeric grind—women back to their homes, children darting between bamboo groves. But now, it was time to meet the one they called Pejari Amma—the elder who carried the spirit songs of the forest and the memory of the Meriahs.

They reached a stone threshold marked with cowrie shells and ash. A sal leaf bowl lay at the base, filled with blackened turmeric roots, dried neem, and something else—soft, ash-white threads, hair perhaps, tied into knots.

Biruka knelt.

"Eliza," he said softly, not looking up, "From here, only one speaks. And one listens."

Eliza nodded and stepped forward.

The hut was small, rectangular, with a thatched cone roof. Inside, in the dim golden light of an oil lamp, sat a woman hunched but regal—her presence vast, like the hill itself. Tattoos curved across her cheeks and forehead like vines that once bled and bloomed into memory. She did not rise. She did not smile.

But her eyes—milky, smoke-colored—narrowed when Eliza sat cross-legged on the floor, knees brushing the old cow dung polish, and bowed her head.

Jitu Mishra

Lika spoke. Her words were slow and wrapped in pauses, as if the forest itself punctuated them. Biruka translated, barely whispering.

"The land remembers all. Even what it has buried."

"Do you come to dig the bones or to bury your name?"

Eliza looked up, startled. But she didn't answer.

She simply opened her journal and closed it again. Then she placed it beside her, untouched.

Lika's gaze finally settled on her face, long and quiet.

Outside, Thomas wandered further than he had ever dared.

His feet found a mossy slope, where a stone slab jutted between two trees. At first glance, it was just another forest marker. But as the sun shifted, he saw the carvings —spiral lines, like the tattoos on Biruka's neck, but etched into rock. A language of curves. Of breath and silence.

He took out his sketchbook, then hesitated.

A small girl stood behind the brush, watching him. She was barefoot, a sliver of turmeric on her chin, her hair tied with red string.

Thomas looked down. Then, instead of drawing, he set the pencil aside and just sat.

He realized he had never felt so quiet.

Jitu Mishra

Back in the hut, Lika began to hum—a tune slow and low, like river stones knocking together. She sang in Kui, and Biruka didn't translate.

Eliza felt something shift inside her chest—a weight she didn't know she was carrying, now lifting like vapor.

When the song ended, Lika reached for a carved box near the wall. She took out a coiled tattooing comb—its teeth dark with old dye.

She held it out—not to Eliza, but to Biruka.

He froze.

"She is asking," he said, voice caught, "if you want to carry our memory."

Eliza didn't reach for it. Not yet.

She turned to Biruka and whispered:

"Tell her I'm still learning the first word."

Lika smiled.

For the first time.

Outside, a wind swept through the bamboo. Somewhere, a drum began to echo faintly in the valley below.

And the forest, old and watchful, listened.

Chapter 7
Signs and Shadows

The Last Meriah

The forest had a way of muting time. Morning light filtered through the tall sal trees in trembling fragments, and the village stirred to the rhythm of grinding stones and birdcalls. Eliza found herself sinking into this rhythm—watching, listening, learning. Yet beneath the surface, something had shifted.

Pejari Amma sang again that morning. She sat beside the fire outside her hut, her blind eyes lifted, her voice rising in lilting verse. The tune was gentle, but the words—translated in hushed whispers by Biruka—gnawed at Eliza's thoughts.

"Daughters of the earth, born of drum and blood,
Their names are carried in smoke.
One shall be taken, not by force,
But by the silence of all."

Eliza sat nearby, cross-legged, her journal in her lap but untouched. She didn't write. She just listened. The song was older than memory, and it brushed against the edges of something she couldn't quite name.

Later, near the stream, she noticed it.

The Meriah girl sat alone under a jamun tree, her thin arms wrapped around her knees. She looked away as Eliza approached. But in that moment, a sleeve slipped down—just enough for Eliza to see the dark blotch near her shoulder. A bruise. Faint, but clear.

"Eliza," Thomas said gently, having seen it too. "We don't know what it means yet."

"But we do know it means something," she replied, eyes fixed on the girl.

The Last Meriah

That evening, Eliza found Biruka sitting on a stone ledge, carving a small wooden figure. He didn't look up when she approached.

"She's not safe, is she?" she asked softly.

Biruka's hand paused. His voice, when it came, was low and firm. "You need to understand. Not all clans agree with what we allow here. Across the northern hills, the Denga line—they follow the old path. They do not want your eyes watching."

Eliza nodded. "They know about her?"

"They've always known. But now they watch more closely."

The fireflies emerged, dotting the darkening woods with sparks of gold. Somewhere far away, a drumbeat began —slow and steady, like the forest's own heartbeat.

"She's been pulling away," Eliza whispered. "As if she already knows."

"She does," Biruka said. "Children always know."

A silence fell between them.

Back in their small hut, Eliza sat beside Thomas in the soft flicker of lantern light. She leaned against his shoulder, not speaking. He wrapped an arm around her, gently. They didn't need words tonight.

Outside, shadows moved. The leaves trembled without wind. And deep in the forest, the drums continued to whisper.

Jitu Mishra

The Last Meriah

Chapter 8
The Bruise Beneath the Skin

The Last Meriah

The rain had not come, and the elders said it was a sign.

By midday, the heat pressed low over the village like an unspoken sentence. The leaves of the sal trees hung limp. Even the birds fell quiet. From her place beneath the neem, Eliza watched as the village moved in slow silence—less like a living community, more like a rehearsal for something solemn.

The Meriah girl had not spoken since yesterday.

Her name, whispered once by Pejari Amma, was Shami. She hadn't cried when the bruises were first seen—one near her shoulder, another, fainter, beneath her collarbone. Her silence was not stubbornness. It was expectation.

Eliza walked toward the grove near the stream, where Shami sat each day beneath the jamun tree. The girl didn't flinch as Eliza approached, but her body shifted slightly—as if preparing to shrink, not flee.

Eliza knelt beside her, slow and without sound. She took her journal from her satchel, opened to a blank page, and wrote in soft strokes:

"Are you hurt by hands, or by rules?"

Shami glanced but didn't read. Instead, she placed her hand over the page and gently closed it.

Eliza swallowed. "Can I help you?"

The girl finally looked up. Her eyes, dark as the earth after rain, blinked once.

Then she mouthed a single word in Kui.

The Last Meriah

"Nani."

Grandmother.

Eliza returned to Pejari Amma's hut, finding Biruka seated in the shade, whittling a figure of a girl with long hair and hollow eyes.

"She doesn't want me near her anymore," Eliza said.

Biruka didn't look up. "That means she knows you see."

That evening, the village elders gathered beneath the large sacred fig. Eliza and Thomas stood at a distance, but the tension reached them in waves.

Biruka joined them after the meeting, his jaw tight.

"They say the forest is angry. The signs are clear."

"What signs?" Thomas asked.

"No rain. Dead sparrow in the bathing pit. A drumbeat heard at dawn that no one played."

He paused. "And... someone painted symbols on the girl's hut last night. The old ones. The ones they used before—when a girl was taken to the grove."

Eliza clenched her hands. "Is that why she's bruised? Are they—preparing her?"

"They say it was the Denga," Biruka said quietly. "The rival clan. From across the hills. They still follow the old rites. They don't like that our village has let her live this long."

The Last Meriah

Thomas took a step forward. "Then we need to do something. Tell them this must stop."

Biruka stood. "To them, you are the reason she hasn't already been taken. And now the Denga say she is... tainted. That if we don't sacrifice her, they will."

Eliza's breath caught. "She's just a child."

"To them," Biruka said, "she's soil returned in skin."

That night, Thomas sat outside their hut, sharpening a stick absentmindedly. Eliza sat beside him, her eyes fixed on the canopy where the moon played shadows through leaves.

"She said 'Nani,'" Eliza whispered.

"She's afraid," Thomas said.

"She's accepting."

Thomas turned to her. "Then you'll have to be the one who doesn't."

Chapter 9
The Council Divides

Jitu Mishra

The fig tree stood at the village's center like an ancient witness. Its roots coiled above the ground like sleeping serpents, and its canopy spread wide enough to swallow a dozen voices. Beneath it, the council had gathered.

Eliza was not invited.

From a distance, she could only see the curved backs of the elders, their heads bowed in tense deliberation. Smoke curled from a low fire between them. At the edge, Biruka stood with arms crossed, unspeaking. His presence alone was a challenge.

"What are they saying?" Thomas asked from behind her.

"I don't know," she said, though her stomach already did.

By midday, the change had spread like heat.

The women who had once laughed beside Eliza at the grinding circle now stepped away when she entered. The playful children no longer ran to touch the hems of her skirts. Even Pejari Amma, resting in her hut, seemed quieter—her songs faded into murmurs, like a drum muffled under a heavy cloth.

At the bathing stream, a young boy walked past Eliza and spat beside her feet.

That evening, Biruka returned from the council.

"They think Shami is no longer fit," he said quietly. "Because you touched her. Because she speaks less now."

"She always spoke less," Eliza replied. "She speaks in silence."

Jitu Mishra

"They say you made her forget that silence has meaning."

Near the fire, Thomas looked up from his journal. "We should leave," he said. "Now. Go to Berhampur. Tell someone. Write to Calcutta if we must."

"And what then?" Eliza asked. "They'll send men with orders? With guns?"

"They'll send someone with power. Which you don't have here."

Eliza's jaw tensed. "They'll call it rescue. But it will be theft."

Thomas stood. "And you? What do you call it when a girl dies because no one dared to interfere?"

The fire popped, casting red sparks into the night. Neither of them spoke again.

At dawn, Eliza stepped outside to find something half-buried in the earth near their door.

A blade.

Small, curved, wrapped in old red thread. The handle was carved with faded spirals and a bird whose beak pointed downward.

She held it up, her breath catching.

Biruka emerged from the shadows of a tree.

"It's not for use," he said. "It's for memory."

Jitu Mishra

"They want her to be afraid."

"They want you to be," he said, his voice flat. "So when they take her, you will not stop them."

That evening, as dusk settled over the village, a figure appeared at the far edge of the fields—a stranger, wrapped in a dark shawl, a curved axe slung across his back.

He stood facing the village for a moment too long.

And then disappeared into the trees.

Thomas stood beside Eliza, his eyes fixed on the fading trail.

"They're not going to wait," he said. "They'll come."

Eliza said nothing. She only looked toward Shami's hut, where a small oil lamp flickered like a heartbeat barely holding on.

Chapter 10
The Kiss by the Forest Shrine

The Last Meriah

They left the village under the cover of moonlight.

Biruka led the way, silent as always, his bare feet knowing which roots to step over and which branches to duck under. Eliza walked just behind him, clutching Shami's small hand, her journal left behind for once. Thomas followed, a lantern swinging low in his grip, throwing long shadows that slipped between the sal trees like memory.

They moved without words—words would have drawn spirits. Or worse, men.

By the time they reached the old forest shrine, the moon had passed its height. The shrine was barely a structure anymore—just four stone pillars and a flat platform draped in moss and offerings long returned to soil. An abandoned brass pot, dried turmeric stains, and a carved figure of Dharani Penu, half-erased by lichen.

"This place," Biruka whispered, "is too old for rules. No clan claims it. That is why it's safe."

He stepped back into the trees.

Shami curled up near the base of a banyan root, her head resting on Eliza's scarf. Her breath was shallow but even. The bruise on her shoulder had darkened into violet.

Eliza wet a cloth from a copper pot beside the shrine and gently cleaned Shami's hands. The girl didn't resist. But she didn't look at her either.

"I don't need you to trust me tonight," Eliza whispered. "Just to rest."

The Last Meriah

Thomas remained at the edge of the grove, lantern in hand, watching the shadows shift beyond the clearing.

Later, they sat by the small fire Thomas had built—just embers now, feeding on twigs. The silence between them was full, but not heavy.

"She's just a child," Eliza finally said.

"I know," he replied.

"She carries everything. Their fear. Their history. Even their future."

Thomas nodded. "You carry some of that now too."

She looked at him, tired but still burning inside. "You know we can't leave her behind."

"I don't want to leave either," he said quietly. "Not because I love this land. But because you're here."

She looked at him for a long time. Her eyes shimmered —not with tears, but with something raw and bright.

She reached for his hand.

He met it halfway.

The kiss came not as a question, but a resting place. Their lips met gently, unhurried—an answer neither of them had needed to speak aloud.

A breeze passed through the grove, stirring the leaves like the breath of the forest.

The Last Meriah

Behind them, Shami stirred slightly in her sleep but did not wake. The carved face of the goddess above her bore no judgment—only time.

From somewhere far away—maybe across the ridge, maybe deeper in the trees—a drumbeat began. Slow, deliberate. Not yet a threat. But not silence either.

Eliza didn't flinch.

Thomas only said, "They'll come soon."

Eliza nodded. "Then let them find us here—holding on."

Chapter 11
The Drum Between Worlds

Jitu Mishra

The forest had turned still. Even the wind seemed to hesitate that morning, as if uncertain of its place in the day.

Eliza rose early, shaken from a dream of water turning to flame. The trees outside shimmered with dew, and in the hush that followed the fading stars, a drumbeat had come — not loud, not frantic, but slow, deliberate. Like a heart announcing itself before being cut open.

She found Shami curled beside the banyan, still sleeping, her cheek against the scarf Eliza had wrapped her in the night before. For a moment, she didn't want to move. The girl's breath was calm, but Eliza noticed something new — her hands had been painted during the night. Smears of turmeric and charcoal outlined a spiral across the back of her right hand.

Thomas arrived with a packet of roasted millets. His shirt was damp with mist. "I saw smoke from the north ridge," he said softly, nodding toward the rival village. "Could be just cooking fires."

Eliza met his eyes. "Or a message."

By midday, the elders gathered again under the banyan tree. This time, the women stood apart, silent but watchful. Pejari Amma sat on her carved stool, her face unreadable. Shami stood beside her now, no longer a child of the crowd but a presence — marked and claimed.

Biruka stood a little behind Eliza and Thomas, tense. His shoulders did not relax as usual when Eliza spoke to him.

"They are speaking of the past," he said in Kui. "The way it was before. They say... the earth drinks or the earth dries."

Jitu Mishra

The phrase shivered through her. "And if the earth is dry?"

"She will hunger," he replied.

Later that evening, Eliza walked alone toward the stream. She needed space. Shami had withdrawn again, barely speaking. The women avoided eye contact. Only a few days ago, she'd felt welcomed. Now she was becoming another question mark in their order.

Then she saw the painted symbol.

It was on a rock by the stream — drawn in red dye and powdered ash: a circle within a spiral, flanked by axe-marks. Not the formal symbol she had documented in her early journals, but something rawer, angrier.

She stepped back and stumbled — only to be caught by a steady hand.

Thomas.

"They're preparing," he whispered.

"For what?"

"I don't think they even know anymore."

She wanted to cry. But instead, she pressed her forehead against his chest. His arms came around her, and they stayed like that, the air heavy with smoke and mango blossom.

That night, from far beyond the ridge, a rival Kondh drum began to beat. It was slower than the village rhythm. Not festive. Not healing.

Jitu Mishra

Biruka stood at the edge of the village with a spear in hand. Not to fight. To wait.

And inside the hut, Shami sat upright — her eyes wide open in the dark.

Chapter 12
The Tree of Threads

Jitu Mishra

The Last Meriah

The tree waited.

At the heart of the village, the old sal tree rose—taller than any hut, older than any living elder. Its bark bore time like tattoos, and hundreds of red threads fluttered from its trunk, each tied for a prayer, a plea, a daughter, a storm. On this day, the village came not to pray, but to decide.

No drums played. No conch blew. The air felt stripped and sharp.

Shami stood in the center clearing, her hands painted, her eyes blank. Two elder women held her arms—not cruelly, not tenderly, but as if holding a basket of fire. Eliza stood at the edge, her throat dry, her fingers stained with ink and ash. Thomas stood beside her, still as stone.

Biruka was called first.

"You walk with the outsiders," said one elder. "Have you forgotten your roots?"

"I remember them," Biruka replied in Kui, "because I walk among the leaves they dropped."

Murmurs. One man spit into the dust.

A second voice called Thomas a spy. Another pointed at Eliza.

"She watches. She records. But she does not understand."

"She teaches the girl to forget."

"She changes the drumbeat."

The Last Meriah

Thomas's fists clenched, but Eliza stepped forward. The clearing went still.

She walked toward the sal tree, slowly, each footfall like a heartbeat in the silence.

She stopped just short of the tree, unrolled her leather journal, and placed it carefully at the base.

Then she turned, lifted her chin, and spoke in Kui—imperfect, trembling, but clear:

"I do not bring death.
I carry memory.
I carry her name in my breath."

She looked at Shami. The girl's lips parted slightly. Her eyes flickered—not fear. Recognition.

Eliza stepped back and folded her hands.

Then Pejari Amma rose.

She had not stood unaided in weeks. Two women held her arms as she shuffled forward, her silver hair glinting like woven moonlight. Her voice, when it came, was rasped—but it spread like fire across hushed faces.

"We once faced hunger. No rains. No fruit. No laughter.
And we gave the earth not blood,
but thread.
Not skin,
but turmeric.
Not flesh,
but memory."

The Last Meriah

She pointed to the girl. "Let her live. Let her live to remember for us what we could not."

A whisper swept the crowd—not speech, but movement. One by one, without command, people stepped toward the sal tree. Each held a thin thread—red, or yellow, or faded. One thread tied meant let her live. Two, let her go.

The elders did not count.

By dusk, the trunk shimmered—braided thick with single threads, fluttering like fireflies.

Shami sat at the foot of the tree.

She looked up.

And for the first time, she smiled.

Chapter 13
The Girl Who Lived

Jitu Mishra

The wind was softer the next morning.

Turmeric smoke curled from clay stoves, and somewhere in the village, a woman began to hum—not the drum rhythm of sacrifice, but a sowing song. It wove through the air like new cloth, tentative and fragile.

Eliza stood beneath the sal tree. The threads tied the day before still fluttered, now sun-dried and restless. Beneath them, her journal remained untouched. No one had burned it. No one had moved it.

They had simply let it be.

Shami sat near the banyan tree, her knees drawn to her chest. She wore a fresh cotton robe—undyed, plain. The paint on her hands had faded into faint ochre lines.

The other girls were gathering at the turmeric grinding circle. They called to her.

She did not answer.

Instead, she stood and walked alone to the stream.

Eliza watched her from a distance—not following, not interfering. Just breathing in the moment of a girl who had survived what had no name.

The rock where the sacrifice symbol had once been painted was clean now—washed by the night's rain. Shami ran her fingers over its mossy surface.

She didn't smile. But she didn't look away either.

Jitu Mishra

In the afternoon, Eliza was summoned to the elder's circle.

An older woman with a milk-white tattoo down her cheek said to her:

"You did not change our belief.
You reminded it of its other name."

Another said:

"The goddess still drinks. But sometimes... from a cup made of thread."

Eliza bowed—not out of humility, but out of something deeper. Belonging, maybe. Or reverence.

Thomas found her near the edge of the grove.

"I've been thinking," he said, leaning on his sketch satchel. "I might return. There's a ship leaving in ten days from Gopalpur. Merriweather's letter was clear— they expect a full report. I've got enough drawings. Notes."

She said nothing.

"I didn't come to live this," he added. "Just to learn."

Eliza stared toward the grinding circle. "I can't leave."

"I know," he said. And he kissed her temple—like someone folding away a page he didn't know how to finish.

Jitu Mishra

At dusk, Shami walked up to them beneath the banyan tree. Her hands were clean. Her face open.

She looked at Eliza, then at Thomas.

"Can I write now?" she asked.

Eliza didn't speak.

She opened her journal and placed it gently in Shami's hands.

The girl didn't write.

She began to hum.

Not the death song.

A new song.

A song with no name.

Chapter 14
The Sketch That Changed

The Last Meriah

The afternoon heat pressed down like a soft hand, firm but not cruel. Thomas sat beneath the half-leaning thatch shade outside their quarters, a stack of yellowing pages in his lap. His sketchbook, once so tidy and precise, now sagged with wear—pages dog-eared, smudged with charcoal, rain marks warping corners like memory folded the wrong way.

He flipped through the earliest drawings: women grinding grain, tattoo patterns on aging skin, a wide-eyed girl with arms crossed too tightly across her chest.

There she was—Shami—sketched from a distance on his second day in the village. Thin lines for her limbs, shadows under her eyes. He had labeled the page in pencil:
"Meriah subject – bruising visible, ceremonial thread, posture defensive."

He stared at the note. The word "subject" recoiled from him now, stiff and bloodless.

Thomas picked up a pencil to strike it out—hesitated— and instead drew a quiet spiral in the margin.

Footsteps on dry earth. He looked up.

Shami stood a few feet away, barefoot, her hair tied back loosely with a strip of cloth. She didn't speak. Just sat down beside him, knees drawn up, fingers sifting dry dust.

She reached out without asking and flipped the sketchbook. Her eyes flicked across the pages until she paused on her own image.

The Last Meriah

"You made my shoulders like they were scared," she said softly, in her halting English.

Thomas didn't respond.

She traced the charcoal line outlining her arm. "I don't feel like that now. That's not me."

He looked at her, then at the drawing. The sketch captured what he had seen, yes—but not who she had become.

"I didn't know you yet," he said.

Shami shrugged gently, more curious than hurt.

"I think," she said slowly, "your hands draw fear fast. But they wait to draw other things."

He sat with that sentence. It was truer than he wanted it to be.

After a while, he turned the page. Took out a fresh sheet. Looked at her—not her eyes, not her scars, but her ease.

She sat cross-legged now, humming a faint melody that Pejari Amma had sung nights before. Her hands rested on her lap. Her mouth tilted into the suggestion of a smile that wasn't meant for anyone else.

He began to draw.

No outlines. No names. Just soft strokes to catch the arch of her back, the looseness of her fingers, the upward curve of her hum.

The Last Meriah

From a distance, Eliza leaned against the banyan tree. She didn't speak, just watched. She knew something was shifting—something delicate, forming quietly like honey dripping from bark.

Later that night, Thomas unrolled his satchel and began folding his older sketches. He paused at the newest one— Shami at ease, humming, the spiral faint in the dirt beside her.

He added it to the very front of his book.

Then, with a silent motion, he zipped the satchel shut— and set it back on the shelf.

He would not carry it to the next place.

Not yet.

Chapter 15
Turmeric and Rainlight

Jitu Mishra

The scent of damp soil and crushed roots drifted through the fields like incense.

At dawn, the Kondh women had begun the turmeric harvest. Bent over the golden veins of the land, their hands reached deep into the earth, fingers seeking the swollen bulbs like midwives feeling for life. Each pull brought a satisfying pop and a burst of spice on the air.

Eliza worked among them, her skirt hem caked in mud, a cloth tied around her forehead to keep sweat from her eyes. Her fingernails were stained yellow, her laughter fuller now—no longer self-conscious.

Thomas stood at the edge of the field, sketchbook in hand. At first.

He tried to draw the rhythm—the way the women moved like a single creature, digging, pulling, tossing. But his pencil stopped when he saw Eliza turn, her face streaked with turmeric dust, her eyes lit with something sun-warm and ancestral.

She waved. "Come help!"

He hesitated. Then placed the sketchbook on a rock and stepped barefoot into the mud.

The women made room. One handed him a spade. Another patted his shoulder, amused by his awkward grip. Eliza stood beside him, her body close but unhurried.

"You'll need to earn your lunch," she teased.

"I'm already earning a legend," he replied, wiping sweat from his brow. "This is how British maps get smudged— yellow hands, distracted hearts."

Jitu Mishra

She laughed. The sound made one of the younger girls glance up and smile.

By midday, the pile of turmeric roots had grown into a small hill. Children ran around it, throwing strands of grass like offerings. The women had begun washing the roots at the stream, their chatter rising like birdsong.

Eliza stood waist-deep in water, splashing clean the stubborn stains.

Thomas sat on the bank, watching. A yellow smear crossed his cheek. His shirt clung to him. He looked like he belonged to the land now—creased, burnished, familiar.

She turned to him, eyes playful. "You look ridiculous."

"I've never felt better," he said.

Later, beneath a neem tree, they rested on woven mats, a bowl of roasted grain between them. Shami lay nearby, curled like a cat, her forehead pressed to her arm.

Eliza reached out and brushed a smear of turmeric from Thomas's wrist. "You didn't sketch today."

"No," he said. "I was too busy... being drawn in."

The pause held. She met his eyes.

Neither moved.

And then the wind changed.

A low rumble rolled across the sky. The air thickened.

Jitu Mishra

Rain.

The first drop hit her cheek like a blessing.

Thomas looked up. "We should go—"

But Eliza stood already, arms open, face turned skyward.

She spun once, soaked in seconds.

And he followed.

They ran, barefoot, laughing, back to the shelter of the banyan grove. Their clothes clung to them, turmeric stains blooming into soft halos. Breathless, they leaned together under the hanging roots, shoulders pressed, laughter trailing into silence.

Eliza touched his arm.

"You're not the same man who arrived in Calcutta," she whispered.

"I'm not sure I ever was."

They said nothing more.

The rain kept falling.

And the turmeric-scented earth held their footprints a little longer than usual.

Chapter 16
Night of the Drum and Dance

The Last Meriah

The sky glowed copper as the last light bled out behind the sal trees. Smoke from evening fires curled gently upward, mixing with the scent of ghee, roasted roots, and palm liquor.

The village had changed.

No one said it aloud, but the moon knew.

Tonight was a festival not born from conquest or conquested gods—but from rain. From turmeric pulled fresh from soil. From girls who had not been buried, but were instead dressed and offered a song.

The drummers gathered near the central fire pit—four men with shoulders streaked in ash, each carrying double-sided dhols tied with turmeric-threaded ropes. The beat began slow, like a remembered heartbeat. Then faster.

Eliza sat with the women, her hands painted with floral motifs, her hair oiled and loosely braided. The elder women had draped her in a deep blue cotton wrap trimmed with red tassels—handwoven, heavy with community.

Shami sat beside her, glowing beneath a necklace of dried gulmohar petals. She had not worn red since her "naming," but tonight, there was red on her lips, in her eyes, in the way she leaned into the drum's rhythm like a girl whose body was once borrowed but had now returned.

Thomas watched from a distance, near the grain baskets. His shirt was unbuttoned at the collar, sleeves rolled to the elbow. He had sketched all day, his pages stained with charcoal and turmeric dust, but now his hands were still.

The Last Meriah

He was no longer drawing Eliza.

He was learning her.

The dance began when the fire hissed its first pop.

Young women formed a circle, arms linked at the elbow. They moved clockwise, hips gently swaying, steps tapping in tight rhythm. A second ring of men began to form around them.

Eliza was pulled in—not ceremonially, but insistently. She laughed, stumbled once, found her footing. Her smile stretched beneath the starlight like a kite finding wind.

Across the fire, Thomas stood alone.

Then a boy of ten grinned and shouted in Kui, "The Englishman has legs!"

The crowd howled.

An elder man walked up and slapped Thomas on the back. "If you can draw our bones," he said in broken English, "you can move them too."

And so Thomas stepped in.

They danced.

Not as performers, not as guests, but as people. Tired, alive, lifted by rhythm.

And then, the drums shifted—their beat slowed, deepened. The men stepped out.

The women stayed.

Jitu Mishra

The Last Meriah

In the center, Eliza stood alone. She looked across the fire to Thomas.

Their eyes held.

She walked toward him, slowly, like the end of a song.

He met her halfway.

And there, at the edge of the embers, they kissed.

Not hidden.

Not ashamed.

Just... home.

That night, they sat apart from the others, beneath the banyan tree. No words. Her head rested on his shoulder. His fingers laced with hers.

Above them, the moon watched.

And for once, did not judge.

Chapter 17
The Tattoo and the Thread

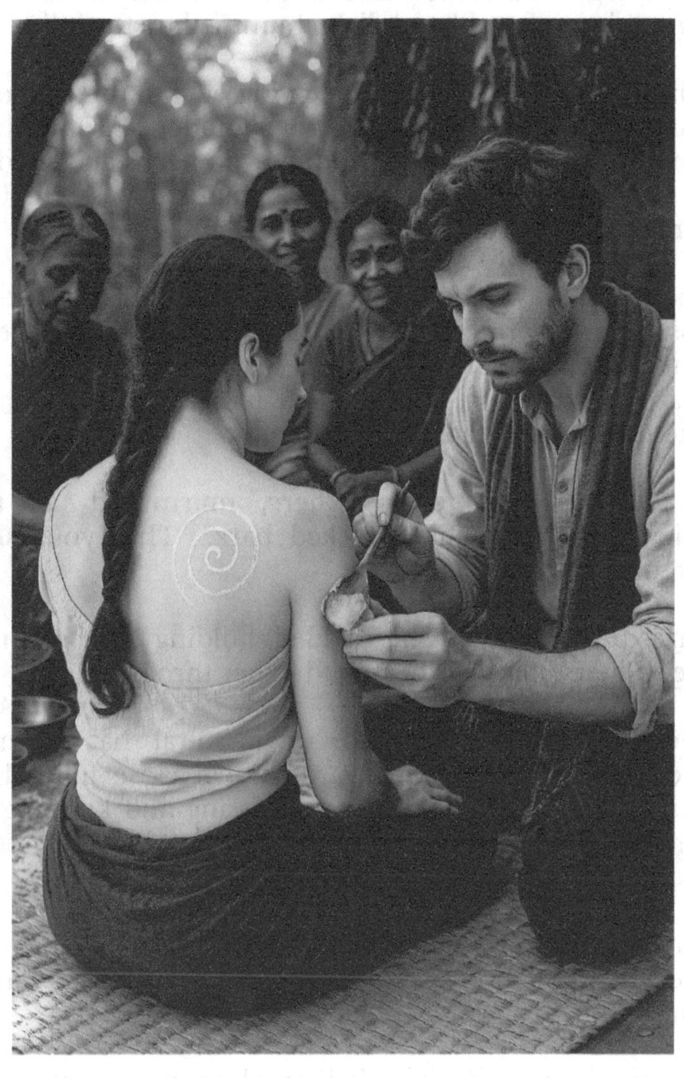

Jitu Mishra

The morning air was thick with the scent of turmeric, ash, and crushed leaves. After the night of fire and dance, the village had settled into a hush — not silence, but something softer, like a lullaby hummed by the hills.

Eliza sat cross-legged in the clearing behind the women's huts, her blouse loosened at the shoulders. Around her, the Kondh women were grinding wild herbs and singing in low, rust-coloured tones — a sound that seemed to come from the soil itself.

Today, they were offering her a marking — not of possession, nor identity, but of presence. A symbolic tattoo, drawn not with needles but with a blend of charcoal, turmeric, and crushed indigo, pressed gently into the skin and fading with time.

"It tells the forest you were here," murmured Aari, the elder with palms like cracked bark. "That your skin listened."

Eliza did not speak. She nodded, holding her breath in the stillness, her heartbeat loud in her throat.

She chose the spiral-thread: a twin spiral that began at two points and coiled inward, drawn close until they touched — a sign of two lives crossing and knotting in time. She pointed to the space just below her right shoulder blade. Aari smiled.

When the paste was ready, the women stepped aside.
"Let the one who walks beside you place the first ring," Aari said with a grin that held stories.

Thomas froze mid-step, a half-laugh escaping him.
"Eliza... are you sure?"
She turned to him, her back bare, the spiral's outline traced in thin chalk.

Jitu Mishra

"I trust you," she said. "It'll fade. Like stories — unless we tell them."

His fingers were clumsy, the turmeric paste slipping off the leaf blade. He knelt beside her, the hut's shadow behind them, and began to press the thick golden dye into the lines, following the spiral with reverence. His hands shook, not from fear but the gravity of the moment — this wasn't anthropology. This was intimacy.

The other women wandered away, leaving the two in their quiet completion.

That night, inside their shared hut, the oil lamp cast lazy shapes on the mud walls. Eliza lay on her stomach, feeling the paste dry and tighten on her skin. Thomas sat beside her, sketching in her notebook — his own awkward version of the spiral, beside a moth, a banyan leaf, and what might have been Eliza's braid.

They laughed — full-throated, foolish laughter — when he tried to draw Shami and ended up with something between a fox and a coconut.

"I'm better with words," he confessed.
"So write something," she said, passing him the charcoal stub.

He did. A sentence, a story beginning — about a boy who came to a forest and met a girl who wasn't trying to be anything but real.

Later, they lay side by side on the floor mat, the world outside fading into cicadas and distant drumbeats. Between them, Shami slept curled like a comma, her tiny hand resting on Eliza's arm — the same arm still tinged with turmeric.

Three lives, no longer separate points in a notebook.
But a thread — tangled, spiraling, held.

Chapter 18
Cracks in the Grove

The Last Meriah

The morning began like any other — mist on the hill ridges, smoke rising from the hearths, Shami drawing lazy spirals in the dust. But by mid-afternoon, a silence had settled over the village — not peaceful, but tight, as if the air had been wrung out and hung to dry.

A delegation from the neighbouring village had arrived. They came without drums, without greetings — only long stares and machetes slung too loosely on their hips.

Eliza stood near the sal tree, her notebook tucked under her arm, Thomas beside her, lips tight. The women who had laughed with them just yesterday were now standing a little apart, their eyes unreadable.

An elder from the visiting group stepped forward — a tall man with a moon-shaped scar across his temple, wearing a thread of woven grass and dried bone.

"You draw our trees," he said in a flat voice. "You listen to our tongues. But whose tongue speaks through yours?"

Before Eliza could answer, a younger man — fierce-eyed, barely more than a boy — stepped forward and pointed to Thomas.

"He walks behind our girls. Watches them. Does he not mark paths for others to follow?"

Thomas opened his mouth, then closed it again. His hands — always steady in camp — twitched at his sides.

"We came to listen. To learn," Eliza said finally. "Not to take. Not to harm."

The elder looked at her for a long time.

"Not all theft is done with blades," he said. "Some is done with ink."

The Last Meriah

Back at the hut, Shami had tucked herself into a corner, eyes wide and still. She did not cry, but she held her wooden bird — the one Thomas had carved for her — so tightly the beak snapped off.

That night, the village fire burned low. No one invited Eliza and Thomas to sit. No bowls of sal rice were handed to them. The Kondh women who had once daubed turmeric on Eliza's back passed by without a glance.

Later, alone in the hut, Thomas lit the small lamp and sat cross-legged, trying to sketch the scarred elder's face — but the lines kept twisting.

Eliza stared at the wall.

"Do you think they're right?" she whispered.
"About what?"
"That I'm a thief with ink."

He didn't answer for a moment.
Then:

"No. But I think they've been stolen from before. And now... they expect it."

She nodded, eyes burning.
Then she laid her head on his shoulder.
They said nothing more. But the silence felt earned, not hollow.

Outside, the wind carried voices from the other side of the forest — drums, faint and uneven. Not a celebration. A warning.

And somewhere between firelight and shadow, the spiral on her back itched — as if it knew the ground beneath them was shifting.

Chapter 19
The Salt and the Ash

Jitu Mishra

By morning, the village fire had been moved. It now burned near the stone circle of the elders — far from the hut where Eliza and Thomas stayed. No one told them they were unwelcome. They simply stopped being included.

Meals were no longer left at their doorway. A pot of rice, once gently delivered by Aari every evening, was replaced by silence. Eliza tried to speak to her once — but the older woman walked past, her eyes fixed on the ground. Shami stood between them, uncertain, then followed Aari without a word.

That evening, a ritual of protection was held in the neighboring village. Eliza watched from a distance — from behind a neem tree where the bark peeled in thin spirals like paper offerings. She saw the smoke rise in coiling lines. Heard the guttural chants. Saw a totem set on fire — one carved in the image of a snake twisted around a banyan.

A message: burn the threat before it strikes root.

When she returned to the hut, Thomas was grinding charcoal with oil, using his finger as a brush.
On the hut wall, he had drawn the elder's face again — the one who had accused them. But this time, the scar across the forehead looked deeper. And behind him, Thomas had added branches instead of hair — as if the man were a tree, too deeply rooted to bend.

Eliza sat beside him without speaking. She was tired of explaining herself to walls that listened but never echoed.

The next day, a young boy from the village — no more than ten — smeared ash on the ground outside their hut, drawing a line across the threshold.

Jitu Mishra

When Eliza stepped out, he said nothing. Just looked at her with fierce, sunlit eyes.

"It's just salt and ash," Thomas whispered behind her. "Maybe it's meant to keep spirits away."
"Maybe we are the spirits now," she replied, and stepped over it.

That night, they didn't light the main lamp. Instead, they lit a smaller oil bowl, and sat shoulder to shoulder. The hut felt smaller, but warmer — not from the fire, but from the way silence no longer felt lonely between them.

Thomas placed his palm gently on her back, over the fading spiral.

"Still there," he said.
"Always," she murmured.

He began to sketch again — not faces this time, but roots. Tangled, exposed, searching.

And Eliza, for the first time since arriving, began to write not in her field journal — but on scraps of cloth with a piece of charcoal. A different kind of story. One not meant for publications. One meant for staying.

Chapter 20
A Path Without Footprints

The Last Meriah

The rains came early that week — not in torrents, but in stealth.
The forest floor turned to sponge. The paths between villages blurred. The bamboo leaves wept without sound.

On the third morning of mist and silence, a cry rang out from the direction of the neighboring Kondh village — the one that had turned its back on Eliza and Thomas.

A child had gone missing. A girl, perhaps six or seven. She had followed a bee, they said. Into the deeper forest. Past the stones no one crossed.

The men gathered in clusters. Some beat drums. Others climbed trees, shouting names. But no one crossed into the eastern trail — a dense pocket the elders said was cursed.

Eliza heard it all from the edge of her hut. She didn't wait.
She slipped on her sandals, tucked a scrap of turmeric cloth into her waist, and whistled low for Shami.

Thomas was already tying a rope around his shoulder, the blade tucked into his bag.

"They won't want us there," he said.
"We're not going for them," she replied. "We're going for the child."

They found her after two hours of weaving through shadowed undergrowth, the sky leaking between canopy branches like melted silver.

She was curled at the base of a tree — her leg scraped, body trembling, eyes wide with something ancient.
Her hands clutched a honeycomb — bitten into, dripping — as if she'd tried to tame hunger by taste alone.

The Last Meriah

Shami was the one who stepped forward.
She offered the broken bird, the one Thomas had mended and wrapped in cloth.
The child took it and began to sob, not with panic — but with release.

By dusk, they carried her back. The drums had stopped. The forest had stilled.
As they approached the village, no one came forward.

But a pair of hands reached out — her mother, wordless with salt on her cheeks.
She took the child and bowed her head low. Then, without meeting their eyes, she turned away.

Eliza and Thomas stood alone again.
No praise. No welcome. No undoing of the ash line.

Only a faint breeze through the dry grain. And a feeling that something had shifted — not visibly, not loudly, but like a root testing new soil.

That night, Shami sat beside the small fire inside their hut, drawing in the dirt with her fingers.

Two spirals.

They began apart.

Turned inward.

Touched.

Then broke.

And just before sleep took her, she drew a single line reconnecting them — not neat, not perfect, but enough.

Jitu Mishra

Chapter 21
The Courage of Quiet Things

Jitu Mishra

Morning came with no rain, only mist. The kind that draped the forest like a whisper, wrapping every tree in stillness. Eliza sat by the doorway, the ash line long faded. No one had redrawn it. But no one had erased it either.

Inside, Shami folded the cloth with the spiral she'd drawn the night before. She placed it inside the old wooden bowl, beside the bird. She said nothing, but her hands moved like prayer — with care, with memory.

Thomas was outside, fixing the hinge on the hut's bamboo shutter. A small thing. But the sound of it — soft hammering, woven with birdsong — gave the day a rhythm.

Around midday, someone knocked.

Not a knock, exactly. A sound — a thud of something placed gently at the threshold.

Eliza opened the door.

There, wrapped in a leaf, was a handful of dried sal flowers and two pieces of flatbread. No note. No words.

She looked around. No one was visible. Only distant movement — a woman in red walking past a goat pen, not looking back.

She carried the offering inside.
Shami's eyes lit up, but she said only:

"Keep it for evening."

That evening, they lit a small fire inside the hut. Not for cooking — just for warmth. For being.

Thomas reached for his sketchbook, then paused.

Jitu Mishra

"What if I never write anything about this?" he said suddenly.
"Then it lives here," Eliza said, tapping her chest. "Where it belongs."

They sat together, their backs against the wall.

Shami placed the bird between them, then curled beside it, eyes slowly closing.

"Will we stay?" Thomas asked.
"For now," Eliza replied. "And maybe for long enough."

The flames danced low, their shadows swaying on the wall — not as warnings or stories, but as quiet things that had nothing to prove.

Outside, someone had drawn two spirals on the earth again.

Connected now.

No one claimed them.

But they glowed faintly under the moonlight, as if the forest itself had drawn them back.

Jitu Mishra

Chapter 22
The Return of the Circle

The Last Meriah

The fog of distrust had not vanished, but it had thinned — like morning mist clinging to sal leaves before lifting. Days passed without words, yet gestures softened. The leaf bundle at the threshold had not been a mistake. It had been a beginning.

Eliza sat near the outer fire pit, peeling turmeric with a worn blade. The scent clung to her fingers — earthy, bright, almost defiant. Across from her, Amma returned from the forest trail, her back straight despite the bundle of roots slung over one shoulder. She didn't speak, but sat beside Eliza, placing a dried sal flower on the edge of the cutting board.

Thomas watched from a short distance, sketchbook in hand, recording quietly — not people, but impressions: turmeric smoke, the geometry of leaf-shadows, the fold of cloth at Eliza's waist. He had learned to witness, not interrupt.

That afternoon, Biruka arrived.

He came not as a guest or messenger, but like rain returning to a droughted pond — sudden, stirring. His feet dusty, a new scar across his brow. He carried a pouch of smoked roots and a single hornet-wing bound in thread — an offering. Without announcement, he sat beside Shami, who was tracing spirals in the dust again. She didn't speak. She just pressed her palm beside his. Spiral and handprint. Wing and child.

In the evening, Amma lit the inner fire again — the one they hadn't dared light since the night of the accusation. The flames danced low, almost shy. She placed turmeric in the embers and hummed a song Eliza hadn't heard before. It rose in notes like roots tasting water after a long dry spell.

Eliza leaned toward Thomas and whispered, "They believe the forest listens before it forgives."

The Last Meriah

Thomas nodded, his voice low. "Then let's keep speaking softly."

And so they did. Not with words, but presence.

That night, a spiral was drawn again outside the hut — not by Eliza, nor by Shami. They found it at dawn: fine, nearly invisible, made from crushed wild turmeric and ash. Two spirals. One thread. Drawn not as protest, but as memory. As hope.

Chapter 23
The Skin of the Earth

Jitu Mishra

It began with a sick goat.

Its breath was thin, its eyes cloudy, its legs trembling from something the villagers would not name. A few believed it had been touched by a restless spirit. Others said it had eaten something it shouldn't — a fruit fallen too early from a poisoned branch. Eliza didn't ask for clarity. She only followed.

She watched as the women gathered near the outer fire circle. Amma stood in the center — no words, only gestures. She handed Eliza a bowl filled with crushed turmeric, neem, and the ash of burnt banyan leaves.

"Not for eating," said Biruka softly behind her. "For remembering."

Eliza knelt without being told. She dipped her hand into the bowl. The paste was warm, alive. She followed Amma's lead and smeared it along the goat's spine, then behind its ears, then a spiral over its heart.

The goat didn't flinch.

The paste soaked into its skin — yellow into white, memory into breath.

When the ritual was done, the goat was left alone in the shade of a drum-root tree. No one spoke of healing. No one declared success. They simply trusted the turmeric would speak louder than doubt.

That night, Eliza lay awake beside the low fire in the hut.

She hadn't written a word.

Her journal was closed. But her fingers still held the scent of turmeric — sharp, grounding. It felt less like pigment now, more like ink drawn from the soil's own veins.

Jitu Mishra

Thomas sat across from her, sketching with his charcoal again.

"You didn't write anything today," he said.
"I did," she answered. "Just not here."
She placed her palm on the floor. The earth, still warm from the day, answered.

Later, as the coals dimmed and shadows climbed the walls, Shami drew a spiral in the ash near the hearth. She didn't look at anyone. She didn't speak.

Biruka, seated nearby, nodded once.

Not in approval — but in recognition.

The spiral glowed faintly, drawn in turmeric dust and firelight.

"That's not a pattern," Amma whispered from the doorway. "That's how the earth remembers being touched."

Chapter 24
The Language of Leaves

Jitu Mishra

The Last Meriah

It was Biruka who called Thomas into the forest — not with words, but with a low whistle and a half-turn of his shoulder. Thomas followed, stepping carefully on the dew-wet roots, past a tree marked with coiled bark strips. No questions. No explanations.

Biruka moved like someone carrying a secret too old for language.

They walked for hours.

Not fast. Not aimless.

At one point, Biruka crouched and pointed at a banana leaf folded and placed against a fallen branch.

"Message," he said, finally.

Thomas nodded slowly.

"From whom?"

Biruka shrugged.

"From the forest. For the one who knows how to read it."

Thomas smiled, unsure if it was a joke or a truth. Perhaps both.

Later, under a broad fig tree, Biruka showed him how certain leaves were arranged near anthills to signal danger — or peace.

"Some spirits don't like speech," he said.
"But they watch the wind. And the leaves it carries."

The Last Meriah

Thomas, for once, said nothing. He took out his notebook and began sketching not objects, but the shadows of leaves — the spaces between, the folds, the pauses. It felt like writing in a dialect he had always misunderstood.

Back at the hut, Eliza sat beside Amma as she sifted dried turmeric slices into a clay pot. Without being asked, Amma began to speak.

"There was once a river that turned yellow — not with disease, not with fire, but with forgiveness. The people had hurt the earth. They didn't say sorry. They simply stopped asking. They walked. They lit fires. They left the water alone. And the river forgave."

Eliza stared at her, lips parted.

"Is that a story?"
"No," Amma replied.
"It's what the turmeric remembers."

That night, Shami drew again — not spirals this time, but leaf shapes.

Some curled. Some torn. Some carefully mirrored like wings.

Biruka watched her from across the fire and murmured,

"She's beginning to write."

And Eliza finally understood — the Kondh didn't write with ink or script.
They wrote with arrangement.
With smoke.
With turmeric.
With placement.

And now, they were letting her read.

Chapter 25
Returning, Not Arriving

Jitu Mishra

The offering began before dawn.

Not with drums. Not with chants. But with movement — the slow rustle of turmeric-soaked cloth, the crack of kindling, the soft thud of hands patting mud into place. Eliza and Thomas joined without asking what was needed. The forest had taught them: you learn by doing.

A path was marked from the hut to a shallow grove where three sal trees grew in a triangle. Leaves had been swept. Stones arranged in a loose spiral. A thread of turmeric water was poured, linking tree to tree.

Amma led. Shami carried a clay pot, her eyes steady. She no longer clung to Eliza's side. She walked her own rhythm.

Biruka stepped forward last.

From around his neck, he unlooped a cord — dark, frayed, worn by years. Attached to it was a boar-tooth charm, its surface etched with fading spiral marks. Without ceremony, he placed it at the base of the center tree.

"It guarded me long enough," he murmured. "Let it guard this."

No one answered. No one needed to.

Eliza placed her palm against the bark. Her spiral tattoo had faded in color but not in heat. For a moment, she imagined the tree breathing — not in or out, but into her.

Behind her, Thomas stood beside Shami, who now traced a spiral on his open palm with her finger. A language without letters. A grammar of touch.

Jitu Mishra

Amma lit a small flame and whispered something to the earth. Not to the gods. To the soil.

As the sun rose and the fireline curled upward, Eliza whispered — not aloud, but inside herself:

"I was never here to arrive."

"I was only ever meant to return."

Chapter 26
Smoke Over the Ridge

The Last Meriah

The scent arrived before the sound. Acrid, sharp — not of burning wood but of cut roots and damp leaves thrown into flame. From the ridge above the grove, smoke curled like a snake disturbed from sleep. The wind, usually mild at that hour, carried whispers laced with gunpowder and iron.

Biruka had felt this once before — not in the body, but in the bones, when the forest's silence no longer belonged to the trees.

Down by the stream, Eliza paused in mid-sentence. She had been asking Amma about the river seeds — small, ash-colored pods strung around the doorway, believed to hold stories of vanished water. But the words dried in her mouth. The air had changed.

Amma didn't look up. Her hand kept stringing the seeds. "They're marking."

"Marking what?" Eliza asked.

"The edge of what's no longer ours."

In the next clearing, the women had gathered without needing to be called. Shami knelt beside the sacred stones, a thin trail of turmeric dripping from her palm onto a curved leaf. No one spoke, but their bodies knew what to do. The spiral was reshaped, drawn longer, stretching outward like arms reaching across an invisible line.

Thomas arrived last. He had been walking toward the ridge when he saw a group of men — not local. Their clothes stiff. Their mouths covered in cloth. They carried no food, no animals. Only a book, a hammer, and something that gleamed like steel beneath wrapped cloth. One man knelt to the soil, scraped it, and sniffed the dust. Then they looked up and made marks on a map.

The Last Meriah

"They're surveying," he whispered when he reached the spiral.

"Not yet cutting?" Biruka asked.

"Not yet. But they will."

That night, the fire crackled with unease. Amma offered no chants. The goat, once healed, lay curled by the post, silent. Shami pressed her back to the wall, her fingers tracing a spiral of ash over and over again on her knee. Eliza sat close to Thomas, watching him write with hurried, uneven strokes.

"What do they want?" she asked finally.

"Timber. Iron. Routes. Obedience."

"And if they don't get it?"

"They'll take it anyway."

Biruka rose and stepped outside. The moon was veiled behind smoke, but he could still see the sacred grove across the narrow rise. Somewhere beyond it, trees were marked — etched not with spirals, but with numbers in blue chalk.

In his palm, he held his old hornet-wing charm. He had tied it again with red thread that morning, though he didn't know why.

He placed it in the crook of the sal tree, near a new spiral drawn by Shami just hours ago, and whispered in a tongue only the trees remembered.

The Last Meriah

"Tell the earth. Tell the bones. Tell the wind to remember."

Then he turned, and walked back into the flickering shadows of home.

Jitu Mishra

Chapter 27
The Line Beneath the Ash

Jitu Mishra

The morning came thick with mist, but not the kind that cooled the skin. It clung instead — dense, carrying with it the scent of scorched bark and damp cloth. Across the ridge, the surveyors had moved on, but what they left behind was a silence the birds refused to break.

Inside the hut, Eliza traced the spiral Shami had drawn the night before. It was smudged now, half erased by sleep or footsteps. But beneath it, where the dust had settled again, she found a fainter spiral, drawn deeper, older — like a shadow left behind by memory.

"She's started drawing over the old ones," Thomas said, watching her from the threshold.

"She's not just remembering," Eliza murmured. "She's burying them."

By midday, a Kondh messenger from the western valleys arrived. His shawl was damp with sweat and flecks of ash. He didn't sit or drink. Just placed a bundle of broken seedpods and a piece of scorched sal bark before Amma.

She took one look, and exhaled through her nose. "They've burned the grove at Kandhuni. Three trees felled. One elder taken."

Eliza blinked. "Taken?"

"Bound. For questioning. They'll call it justice. But the grove was marked. They knew."

No one asked who "they" were.

Jitu Mishra

That night, the community gathered without fire. The grove stood in stillness — no drums, no chants. Just the rustle of leaves as women laid flat stones in a pattern that no longer spiraled but radiated — outward, like spokes from a wheel, or veins from a wound.

Biruka stepped into the center. He carried no weapon. Only a satchel of turmeric and a feather dipped in river-sap. He knelt, pressed the feather into the dust, and began to draw.

Not a spiral.

A line. Straight. Firm. Drawn west to east.

Thomas inhaled. "That's a border."

Biruka did not speak. He simply nodded once, toward the trees.

Later, Thomas and Eliza sat in the hut's shadow, knees touching, saying nothing. On the mat between them, Eliza opened her journal and slowly, carefully, drew what Biruka had drawn. A line.

Then she whispered, not quite to him:
"What happens when they cross it?"

Thomas didn't answer.

But in the distance, beyond the sal grove, a single hornet cry split the night.

Chapter 28
Roots and Wounds

Jitu Mishra

The Last Meriah

The crack of the axe rang out before the morning birdsong.

It came not from deep within the forest, where the logging was officially sanctioned, but from just beyond the turmeric line — a single sacred tree, its roots long intertwined with birth rituals, songs, and ashes of the dead. A flame-tree, scarlet in bloom, now trembling in death.

Eliza heard the sound first — a dull knock, then a splintering. She rose abruptly, almost stumbling over her journal. Outside the hut, a haze of dust blurred the edge of the grove. Thomas had already stepped out, boots loose, shirt unbuttoned. Neither spoke.

Through the trees, they saw the scene unfold like a myth unraveling: two laborers hacking at the base of the flame-tree, and behind them, a British officer chewing on a twig, impatient.

And then — Biruka's roar. It came not from his throat but from somewhere deeper, older.

He surged forward barefoot, arms outstretched, his body covered in ash and streaks of turmeric. Before the second axe could fall, he struck — not with a weapon, but with his body, knocking one of the laborers to the ground. A scuffle. The officer shouted. A rifle butt crashed into Biruka's ribs. He crumpled but did not break.

Thomas instinctively moved forward, but Eliza held him back. "Let it happen," she whispered hoarsely. "It's already begun."

The Last Meriah

They arrested Biruka.

Bound him with rough rope, dragged him to the outpost by the ravine. He did not resist. Blood oozed from a wound above his eyebrow, where the rifle had kissed bone. Still, he held his gaze steady — toward the broken tree, the shivering leaves, the scattered petals.

Thomas followed them, torn between role and conscience. In the officer's tent, he demanded an explanation.

"That tree was beyond the permitted perimeter. You knew that."

The officer shrugged.

"Survey lines were redrawn yesterday. Paperwork's clean."

That night, Thomas sat in silence, the fire flickering low. In his lap lay an old report from Calcutta — the official decree that ended Meriah sacrifice a decade ago. At the time, it had seemed just. Humane.

But now he saw it differently. The ban on ritual had not ended violence — it had relocated it. Pulled it from ceremony into silence, from symbol into subjugation. The ritual was never about death — it was about balance. Without it, the bond was broken. The forest had become wood. The people, surplus.

Eliza wrote by lamplight.

The Last Meriah

The ink trembled slightly as the monsoon breeze teased at the edges of her paper. She wrote not as an observer, but as a witness:

"They have severed the tree that birthed their children's names.
They have shackled the one who once bled for the land.
We are not watching history. We are watching forgetting."
— Letter to L. R. Sharma, Calcutta Daily Chronicle, unsigned.

She sealed it before dawn. Gave it to a traveling salt vendor headed east.
"Give it only to the man with the red ink on his thumb," she said. The vendor nodded, not asking questions.

At the edge of the grove, Amma lit a small flame under a stone shelf.

No buffalo stood beside her. No child bound with flowers. Only leaves — and silence. The elders gathered, some sitting, some standing, all watching.

Amma began to chant — old songs, fragments of lullabies and mourning cries, stitched with new words.

Shami brought turmeric and rubbed it along the base of her grandmother's feet.

Eliza watched from behind a sal tree, notebook tucked to her chest. She didn't sketch. She just watched.

One by one, the Kondh elders came forward, not to offer sacrifice — but to lay down small bundles of bark, dried honeycomb, and hair from their combs.

Jitu Mishra

Amma spoke only once:

"We remember what they forgot.
We do not offer blood.
We offer memory."

Thomas knelt beside Biruka the next morning, helping clean the wound. The gash above his eyebrow had swelled, purple with defiance. Eliza brought turmeric paste and pressed it gently against the skin.

Biruka flinched, then allowed it.

Eliza paused, fingers stained yellow. Then, slowly, she dipped her finger into the remaining paste and drew a spiral — not on the ground, but next to the wound, wrapping around the bruised skin.

Later that night, Thomas found her sketch.

In her journal, the same spiral reappeared — this time around a tree stump, with small annotated symbols: blood, ash, memory, breath.

Underneath, a question she hadn't yet asked aloud:

"What happens when the forest remembers before the empire does?"

He closed the journal gently. Outside, the cicadas sang louder than the wind.

Chapter 29
The Spiral Reborn

Jitu Mishra

The Last Meriah

It began at the old Meriah grove, where blood once soaked the roots.

But this time, there was no child bound with garlands. No buffalo snorting in ritual defiance. No drumbeat to summon sacrifice.

Instead, a circle of quiet bodies — elders, women, children, even a few boys who once scoffed at ceremony — sat cross-legged around a bare patch of earth. In the center: a slow hand moved in silence, sprinkling turmeric in a spiral.

No chant. No priest.

Just Amma, eyes half-closed, letting the spiral unfurl like breath — one motion, then another. She didn't look up. She didn't need to.

The air held its breath.

Eliza didn't sketch right away.

She stood at a distance, notebook pressed to her chest, spine against a sal tree. She could hear the soft rustle of bark bundles being laid down — small offerings: strips of comb, twisted threads of hair, broken seed husks. Memory, not martyrdom.

Shami's hands trembled slightly as she carried a lump of honeycomb to the edge of the turmeric curve. She didn't place it. She nestled it — as if tucking a memory into soil.

Thomas sat beside one of the elders, watching the smoke from a resin bowl curl upward into the twilight. It veiled the trees like mist returning to its roots.

Jitu Mishra

The Last Meriah

"What is it?" he whispered.

The elder beside him didn't answer immediately. Then:

"The beginning," he said. "Again."

That night, the spiral spread.

First outside the forest office — painted with ash and turmeric on the wall. Then on the backs of metal signboards, where it glowed faintly under dew. One appeared on the colonial boundary map nailed to the old tamarind tree — a spiral drawn in reverse, looping inward instead of out.

"A remembering that folds in," Eliza wrote in her journal.
"As if the land is trying to recall itself."

She found a scrap of charcoal near her bedside — probably dropped by Thomas — and smeared her fingertips with it, drawing spirals on her palms. She pressed one onto the inside cover of her journal, letting the ink bleed into the grain.

The youths began to move differently.

They no longer gathered in defiance. They dispersed — into the woods, into the supply lines, into the very maps drawn by the colonial surveyors. They didn't burn wagons or sabotage tracks. They simply shifted markers, misled patrols, and rerouted signs. A trail here disappeared. A pile of stones turned up elsewhere.

"The jungle bends when it breathes," one boy said with a grin.

The Last Meriah

A British officer reported:

"The men are hallucinating trails. It's as if the forest is... moving."

The colonial camp increased its patrols. Suspicion grew. A rumor began to fester:

"They're planning something. The spiral means revolt."

One night, Eliza and Thomas were invited to a second ritual.

This time, no turmeric. No offerings. Just a bowl of water passed from person to person. Each whispered a name into it — names of lost children, silenced elders, forgotten trees. The bowl trembled slightly, as if echoing their breath.

Thomas sketched the bowl, the hands, the soft shadows on each face.
He titled it: "A Living Archive of Grief."

The crackdown came silently.

Two young men were taken from their huts and not seen again.

A spiral was later found carved into the wooden wall of their detention tent.

On the third day, chalk marks appeared on Amma's hut. A white "X."
Eliza rubbed it away with turmeric water.

That evening, she placed her sketch — the inward spiral — at the grove, tucked beneath a stone.

"Let them think it's a symbol," she said aloud to the dark. "We know it's a memory with teeth."

Chapter 30
No One Will Be Taken

The Last Meriah

At dawn, a hush hung over the grove.

Mist curled around the roots of the sal trees like breath unwilling to rise. The spiral of turmeric from the night before had faded slightly, scattered by wind, but its imprint still held. At its center stood a simple ring of stones, laid by children's hands.

Amma had woken before anyone, her voice a murmur in the dark:

"It is today."

They arrived with spades and rifles.

Three soldiers. Two forest officials. A junior British officer with a hard brow and ink-stained fingers, carrying an order rolled under his arm.

"This ground is unregistered. We've orders to clear it. The stones will be removed. The pole will be taken in for cataloguing."

The younger Kondh men stepped forward instinctively — but Amma raised one hand. Shami ran to stand beside her, carrying nothing but a brass bowl filled with river water and turmeric petals.

One by one, the villagers stepped into a circle. Not to block, not to fight — but to stand. Shoulder to shoulder. Eyes steady.

Biruka limped into the grove last.

The Last Meriah

He wore his oldest shawl — frayed, faded, still streaked with old ritual ash. Around his neck: the boar-tooth charm that once belonged to his father. In his hand: a broken piece of the old Meriah pole, carried from a secret hiding place near the ravine.

He walked past the soldiers, past the officer with the decree, and stopped before the spiral.

Without a word, he placed the charm on the broken pole and laid it at the center of the stones.

Then he looked up.

"You took our blood," he said.
"You cannot take our breath."

The officer raised his hand, signaling the men behind to move.

But Thomas stepped forward, voice shaking slightly.

"Sir, I've documented this grove. The stones are symbolic only. No rebellion. No violence. Just remembrance. What you see is not sedition — it's survival."

The officer's eyes narrowed.

"Are you defending this ritual?"

"No, sir," Thomas said. "I am witnessing it."

Eliza moved beside him, clutching her journal.

"This is not yours to interpret. Let it be."

The Last Meriah

For a long moment, no one moved.

Then the officer lowered his hand.

"Leave it," he said. "We'll return with clarity. And higher authority."

They left in silence, boots cracking through the underbrush.

Shami knelt beside the spiral and poured the bowl of turmeric water slowly over the stones. The yellow bled into the dust, spreading like light.

Amma stepped forward last.

Her fingers trembled, but her voice did not.

"We do not offer Meriah again.
We offer our courage.
And our breath."

As twilight fell again, the grove stood quiet.

No blood. No buffalo. No priest.

Only the faint glow of turmeric, a charm tied to the cracked wood, and the circle of stones.

Eliza sketched it in silence. Thomas wrote nothing. Shami sat with her head on Amma's lap. Biruka stood behind them all, arms crossed, gaze unblinking.

A breeze stirred the dust.

From the canopy above, a single petal fell — not red, but white — and landed in the center of the spiral.

Jitu Mishra

Chapter 31
The New Meriah

Jitu Mishra

For weeks after the standoff at the grove, the village moved gently, as if afraid to stir something sacred that still hovered in the trees. No one touched the stones. The spiral faded but was not forgotten. People came quietly, not in mourning, but in memory.

The rains, however, stayed away.

Turmeric shoots were weak in the podu fields, and the earth, once full of promise, began to crack at the edges. Baskets returned light from the hills. Hunger didn't cry out, but it moved beneath everything — in sighs, in silent glances, in the dry pulse of the soil.

Then one morning, the Dehuri called the elders.

No summons was sent, yet everyone came. They gathered at the southern ridge, where the land opened into soft red earth. This place had no name. It didn't need one. It was where turmeric remembered how to bloom.

The Dehuri stood tall, his body wrapped in an ochre cloth, cowries resting on his chest like seeds. His eyes, half-shadowed by the rising sun, searched the horizon before speaking.

He said nothing of the grove. He spoke only of roots, of withering harvests, of spirits who waited. And of a buffalo — dark as rainclouds, born under a waning moon, kept from yoke or burden. The beast had already arrived, unbound, standing calmly at the field's edge. It had not been pulled. It had come.

"We ask the land for breath," the Dehuri said. "But the land, too, asks for strength. This year, we give it a body born of us — but not from us."

Jitu Mishra

There were no protests. Even Shami stayed silent. Not in agreement, but in knowing.

Later, as the sun climbed higher, the drinking began. Mahula passed in leaf cups, warm and rough. Feet started to move. First slow, then quick, then wild. Men and women spun, shoulders bare, voices rising in fractured song. The children joined in, streaked with turmeric and soot, their laughter cutting through the chant like bright threads in old cloth.

The buffalo stood still in the center of it all, garlanded and silent.

Eliza stood at a distance, notebook closed. Some things were not for writing. She watched the spiral return in a different form — not drawn on the earth this time, but danced with feet, spilled in drink, echoed in the throats of people who sang with salt and soil in their breath.

Later, she found a folded cloth on her cot.

Inside was a single turmeric bulb, still moist with earth, wrapped in a thin strip of buffalo hide. No name. No message. She opened her journal and pressed it there, then wrote quietly below:

"No blood in the grove.
But the earth still drinks.
The spiral continues — in harvest."

The next day, Thomas walked with Biruka to the edge of the fields. The soil had been turned. Women moved gently between rows, planting. Their fingers pressed small pieces of flesh — not much, just enough — into the spaces between the turmeric roots. Not with ritual, not with mourning. With memory.

Jitu Mishra

A young girl smeared turmeric on her forehead and ran laughing toward the ridge.

Thomas said nothing.

Biruka, watching the field, murmured, "The gods... they learned mercy. But the land—" he paused, eyes narrowing with something older than sorrow—"the land still remembers."

Chapter 32
The Deeper Forest

They drew lines on paper.
We drew spirals in dust.
One vanished in rain.
The other remained underfoot.
— Kondh saying, remembered

The Last Meriah

No one returned to the grove.
Not the officers.
Not even the wind.

But they came for the forest.

Not with rifles or drums this time, but with leather-bound ledgers and iron-tipped survey poles. Three British men, led by a quiet officer with a ring on his thumb, arrived with their assistants and guides. They walked softly, yet everywhere. Every path became a straight line. Every tree a potential number. Every hill a future road.

They never said the word Meriah. Not once.
They spoke instead of "productivity."
"Excess growth."
"Administrative clarity."

By the fourth day, white chalk slashes began to appear — quick, careless cuts across the bark of sal and neem. Some marks landed on trees near ancestral shrines. Others appeared at the edge of the turmeric fields. One tree, marked twice, stood beside the spring where women gathered each morning — the same place where Amma once whispered her last chant.

Thomas found the new map rolled tight on the veranda of the outpost. He opened it slowly beneath the amber light of dusk.

The new boundary crept like a vein through the land — bold red lines severing old pathways. Podu fields were relabeled as "encroachment." Sacred groves became "unclassified compartments."

Eliza leaned in beside him. Her breath smelled faintly of ash and rice.

The Last Meriah

"What do they call the grove now?" she asked.

He pointed to a square just beyond the river bend.

"Reserve Block 9B."

She didn't reply.
She folded the map and slid it behind a thatch mat, as if placing it far away from breath.

That night, they moved without fire.

Biruka led the way. His shawl was tied high. Behind him walked elders and youth, silent, carrying pouches of turmeric paste and handfuls of ash.

They visited each tree that bore the white slash.

One by one, they wiped the chalk away. Then, using finger and cloth, they pressed a spiral in its place — soft, invisible from far, but unmistakable up close. Ash curled into turmeric like memory into ritual.

At the spring, Shami knelt beside the marked trunk. She tied a single red thread around it, her lips moving without sound. Then she stood, and walked back without looking behind.

Eliza watched from the shadows and did not sketch.

In the morning, the timber team returned.

They found the marks gone, replaced by faint spirals they didn't understand.

The officer frowned, but gave no order.
Not yet.

Jitu Mishra

Over the next days, the air shifted.

Shami began gathering the younger girls in a half-circle outside Amma's hut, long before the sun reached the ridge. They sat on the earth, silent at first. Then one would hum a phrase — a broken chant, a piece of an old song — and the others would repeat it until their breath braided it back into rhythm.

One morning, Shami stood. Her voice was quiet, but unwavering.

"We are not here to remember death," she said.
"We are here to remember how to walk where others say we cannot."

Eliza no longer wrote everything down. Some things she stitched instead — spirals dyed into strips of cloth, one for each girl. She used turmeric and soot, the same materials the land gave back. She no longer asked permission to make meaning.

Thomas kept mostly to himself. He began writing, not reports but reflections. Letters without addresses. Sentences with no salutation. At the top of one page, he had written:

"If empire is a sentence, perhaps silence is punctuation."

One evening, they met beneath the hornet-wing tree.
The wind was still. The wing barely moved.

Eliza sat on the stone. Thomas leaned beside her.

They didn't speak at first.

Then she said, "If they cut the spring, they won't just take water. They'll take names."

Jitu Mishra

He nodded.

"They'll call it development."

She didn't reply.

Instead, she reached into her satchel and pulled out a bundle of cloth — her spiral folio. Inside were sketches, chants, fragments of songs, names of trees, voices of children, drawings of hands. She didn't open it. She just held it out.

"This is what we keep," she said. "If the trees fall. If the voices are forgotten. If they redraw the world."

Thomas didn't take it. But he didn't look away.

"If we fall," he whispered, "let them at least know we once stood in a circle."

The next morning, a new survey team arrived at the eastern ridge.

Before they could plant a single pole, they found the clearing already filled — not with weapons or shouting, but with women on their knees, pressing turmeric bulbs into the soil.

Shami stood at the center, hands stained yellow, planting slowly, as if every root was a story. The spiral was not marked — it was planted.

One of the officers stepped forward.
She didn't move.

She said only:

"The ground is already full."

No one replied.

The Last Meriah

Chapter 33
Kondh Meli

Jitu Mishra

"They took our sacred.
Now we gather not to pray,
But to remember we are many."
— Whispered at the forest's edge

The Last Meriah

It began with silence — not the silence of fear, but the dense, watchful kind that gathers before thunder. Across the hills, through the turmeric fields and under the mahua trees, messages moved without paper. A twisted leaf here. A soot-marked stone there. In the forests, word spread: Meli.

The gathering would be held near the old Meriah grove — the same space once desecrated, now reclaimed. But this was not a festival. This was a reckoning.

They came in twos and threes, men and women from distant valleys, young ones with faces streaked in red earth, elders draped in old cloths daubed with ash. Some carried wooden staffs carved with birds and spirals. Others bore nothing but memory.

At the grove, a ring of torches had already been lit. Not bonfires — signal flames, facing the ridges.

There were no songs of welcome. Only the sound of feet pressing dust, and the crackle of twigs breaking under weight long carried.

Shami stood apart at first, watching the faces arrive — strangers and kin alike. Her eyes searched the circle, counting not names, but resolve.

When she stepped forward, the murmur quieted.

"They thought Meriah was all we had," she said.
"They thought if they could ban one rite, we would forget the forest was our body."

She raised a handful of turmeric, letting it fall in a spiral onto the earth.

"But we are still here. And we know how to remember."

Jitu Mishra

The Last Meriah

Around her, others stepped forward — placing honeycomb, feathers, soil from their fields. Not to sacrifice — but to mark presence. The spiral grew from their offerings, not from blood.

Biruka stood next, his arm still bandaged, his shawl frayed. He spoke no words — only knelt, placing his remaining boar-tooth charm at the base of the spiral.

Behind him, a woman raised a cloth spiral banner, hand-dyed in ash and turmeric. Another unfurled a scroll — a forest notice, banning gatherings — and held it to the torch until it curled in flame.

Eliza and Thomas stood together, wordless. This was no place for sketches. It was a moment to witness.

An elder approached Eliza and pressed something into her hand — a folded piece of cloth, warm from being held.

"You've been writing our stories," she said.
"Now wear one."

Eliza looked down. A spiral, stitched in red thread, pulsed against the cloth's weave.

She tied it at her waist without speaking.

As the night deepened, three boys ran to the ridge's edge and lit torches of their own, facing out toward the valleys.

From the shadows came a chant — not sung, but spoken. Line after line, old cadences newly sharpened:

The Last Meriah

"We are the ones who plant
without asking.
We are the ones who bury
without forgetting.
We are the ones
who gather again."

The Meli ended not with firecrackers or speeches, but
with a vow drawn in dust.

Before dawn, they were gone. Only the spiral remained
— half-washed by dew, but rooted like breath in the soil.

Jitu Mishra

Chapter 34
The Red Line

Jitu Mishra

The mist had barely lifted when the men arrived.

They did not come with announcement or apology.
Just ropes, saws, and silence.
Four British officers, three contractors, and a column of
guards who didn't meet anyone's eyes.

No one had expected them to return so soon after the
Meli.
But they did.
Not to speak. Not to ask.
Only to mark, measure, and cut.

The sal tree stood near the stream, older than memory.
Amma used to sit beneath it in the evenings, grinding
neem leaves with a stone and humming chants that no
one fully remembered.
Children had tied grass ropes to its lower branch and
swung with shrieks.
Its roots had cracked the earth like veins reaching for
sky.

Now it bore a thick white mark. Fresh. Final.

The first sound of the saw cracked through the grove like
a snapped oath.

No one moved.

Eliza stood with her hands frozen around her journal.
She did not write. Shami reached for Biruka's arm, but
he was already walking toward the edge of the grove.

They did not shout. They did not plead.
They watched.

Jitu Mishra

The tree groaned once — then again — and fell.
Its crash was not just sound.
It was a silence broken open.

Dust rose. Leaves flew. A bird fled.

The forest exhaled something it could not take back.

Shami walked into the clearing and dropped to her knees beside the stump.

Her hands pressed into the earth, deep and shaking.
No sob escaped her, but her body carried the sound.
Eliza crouched beside her, placing a hand on her shoulder, then on the soil.
It was warm.

She gathered a piece of bark — rough, damp, and veined — and wrapped it in the edge of her cloth. Later, she would press it into her journal, between two blank pages.

Amma arrived without a word.

She carried no offering, no lamp. Only a bundle of turmeric leaves and wildflowers.
One by one, she handed them to the women who had followed her.
Then she walked barefoot in a slow spiral around the stump.
The others followed — in silence.

Eliza stepped back and watched the circle form — not tight, not perfect. Just human and whole.

No chants. No fire. No old rites.
Just motion.
And memory.

The Last Meriah

Jitu Mishra

Thomas found his superior that evening at the outpost, sipping from a tin cup.

"You've cut a sacred tree," Thomas said.

The officer looked at him blankly.

"Sacred?"
"It was interfering with timber demarcation."

Thomas said nothing for a long moment. Then quietly:

"You do not manage a forest.
You only measure its fall."

That night, he began a report — not for the archives, but for the public.
No signatures. No emblems. Just words.

The rain came before dawn.

Soft at first, then thick, warm, and constant.
It washed the dust from the roots, the chalk from the fallen branches.

The villagers stood again in silence at the grove.

Shami reached down.
Where the tree had stood, the soil had shifted.
In that red earth, a small green shoot was rising — slender, unsure, but unmistakably turmeric.

No one said a word.

But Eliza wrote later:

"They drew a red line through bark.
But the root refused to forget."

The Last Meriah

Chapter 35
The Archive That Cannot Burn

Jitu Mishra

The Last Meriah

The stump no longer bled. Rain had washed the sap away, leaving only the dull sheen of exposed rings — time turned inward. Around it, the grove was quiet. No birds called. Even the cicadas seemed to hush.

In the evenings now, the villagers gathered not for decision, but for remembrance.

They sat in loose circles — no leader, no chant — and the words came slow, like stories drifting from the smoke of cooking fires. Amma did not instruct. She remembered aloud. Biruka would close his eyes and listen. Others nodded, added, corrected gently. The younger ones fidgeted at first, then settled.

Shami did not speak much. But she listened with a kind of stillness that drew others closer.

One night, when the moon sat thin and tilted above the sal canopy, she took a small group of girls to the clearing where the turmeric shoots had sprouted. With a thread of ash and oil, she drew a spiral on her forearm. Then she held the girl's hand and guided her finger over it.

"Not to copy," she whispered.
"To carry."

They repeated it. On arms, on backs, on the soft belly of a gourd. Spirals pressed into river clay. Spirals drawn with neem leaves. Spirals that would vanish by morning — but not before memory passed hand to hand.

The next day, Eliza tried to write it all down. She sat by the grove, journal open, scratching quick notes.

But every time someone repeated a chant, the rhythm shifted. A name was added. A bird's call woven in. A joke slipped in the middle like a hidden root.

The Last Meriah

She looked at Thomas, frustrated.

"It won't stay still," she said.

He smiled, watching the children draw spirals into the dust with their toes.
"Then maybe it's not supposed to."

That evening, Eliza closed her journal. Instead, she sketched — not people, but gestures. A hand curving over an earthen pot. A woman's ankle moving clockwise through turmeric dust. The shape of breath when Amma spoke of her mother.

She stopped recording to remember. And in remembering, began to witness.

One morning, Shami arranged a ring of half-dried mud bricks in the grove. She dipped her fingers in turmeric paste and pressed spirals — gently, slowly — into the center of each.

"Why bricks?" someone asked.

"So we don't forget where we stood," she said.
"And one day, these will hold fire."

She looked toward Eliza, not smiling but sure. "Even your paper can burn. But this... this goes under the cooking pot."

Later that week, a small boy drew a double spiral in the dirt with a mango twig. No one had shown him. No one stopped him.

Amma, lying on her mat near the stump, heard the giggles and turned slightly.

"He remembered it without hearing," she murmured.

Jitu Mishra

The Last Meriah

"That is when story becomes seed."

On the seventh day, the grove smelled of fresh leaves and woodsmoke. The girls gathered around Amma, resting. One of them asked, half-afraid to break the hush:

"Amma... will they ever write it down?"

Amma didn't open her eyes. Her voice was a thread in the breeze.

"Why should they?"
She turned her face to the earth.
"The hills remember.
And your tongue knows the way."

Chapter 36
Spirals Not Drawn

Jitu Mishra

"What the forest accepts, the world cannot refuse."

The forest wore a hush that morning. Not silence, but a kind of softness — a pause between stories. The Meriah grove, where once boundaries were drawn in fear and blood, now shimmered with turmeric dust, laughter, and sal leaves.

No one called it a marriage. No drums announced it, no priests invoked it. Yet it was all there — the solemnity, the intimacy, the thread of something old wrapping itself around something new.

Amma sat under the grove's largest tree — not the one that had fallen, but another, younger, with leaves still learning to shade. Shami stood beside her, holding two cloths: one dyed in turmeric, the other in soft grey ash. The old Dehuri had nodded his blessing at dawn and retreated without words. This was not his to perform.

The villagers gathered in a wide, breathing circle. In the center, Thomas stood — awkward but still, his eyes not on the crowd but on Eliza, who approached slowly, barefoot, her journal absent for the first time.

Children had drawn a spiral in the dust with their toes. Not perfect, not deliberate — just instinct.

Shami stepped forward, and with a leaf dipped in turmeric paste, she pressed a mark on both their foreheads. No chant followed. Only the wind in the leaves and the crackle of a fire kindled not for sacrifice, but for warmth.

Biruka handed Thomas a carved stick — spiral, sun, water, tree — all etched into its length. A guide, not a weapon.

Amma tied the ash-and-turmeric cloths together — not tightly, just enough for them to know they were bound.

Jitu Mishra

And then, nothing.

No kiss, no applause.

Just the villagers beginning to sing — a soft, wordless hum that rose and faded like mist. Eliza leaned into Thomas. He took her hand.

The spiral wasn't drawn that day.

It walked.

Chapter 37
The Departure

"To walk away is not to forget.
It is to trust that the spiral will continue
without you."

The Last Meriah

The forest did not change when Eliza and Thomas announced they would leave. The wind still passed through the sal leaves. The turmeric flowers still bloomed in bursts of yellow flame. But something quieter had shifted — as if the trees now knew they were being watched for the last time by familiar eyes.

It was Shami who spoke first.

"If you stay longer, the forest will never let you go."

Eliza smiled gently. "We'd stay. But this is your song now."

There was no ceremony of farewell. That wasn't the Kondh way.

Instead, they were given tasks — final gestures.

Eliza sat for hours with Amma, helping organize her bundles of sal seeds and bark slivers. She listened to the old chants one last time, not as a student, but as kin.

Thomas spent his mornings retying the bamboo thatch on the roof of the gathering hut, his hands working without urgency. In the evenings, he walked with Biruka — sometimes speaking, sometimes just listening to the footfall on earth.

On the third day, Shami brought out the spiral cloth — the one she had stitched herself with turmeric and ash threads. It was faint now, smudged from months of use.

She handed it to Eliza, pressing it into her arms.

"You carry what you can," she said.
"The rest stays here."

The Last Meriah

Then she turned to Thomas. From her shoulder, she unpinned the woven necklace of seeds Amma had worn in her youth — red, black, and pale grey — and looped it over his neck.

"For remembering the names of things," she said. "Not in your language. In ours."

They left on foot, walking down the narrow trail that led out of the valley. Behind them, no one waved. Instead, the villagers stood quietly in a semicircle. At the center, Amma, seated beside the young sal sapling planted in the heart of the Meriah grove.

As they passed the last bend, Eliza looked back. Just once.

Shami stood alone now, facing the rising sun, her arms folded, her face unreadable. But her eyes were not heavy.

They were watching forward.

Later, on the edge of the town, a stranger asked Thomas if he had found what he came for.

He paused.

"No," he said. "But I became part of something I didn't come to find."

That night, they slept in a rest house near the river. In the courtyard, Eliza unrolled the spiral cloth and pressed it against the earth.

The wind moved through the neem leaves above. She whispered into the dark:

"This is not goodbye. Just a planting."

Jitu Mishra

The Last Meriah

Chapter 38
The Grove Without Trees

Jitu Mishra

The Last Meriah

Their London flat was small — just two rooms above a watchmaker's shop on a narrow cobbled street that rarely saw sun. Yet within its faded wallpaper and creaky floors, something larger than any forest was taking root.

Eliza sat by the window, the same way she used to sit near the grove's edge — quiet, listening. Her journal now filled the room: pages pinned on walls, charcoal sketches tucked into books, dried sal leaves pressed between newspapers. A piece of turmeric-dyed cloth hung above the desk — stained, worn, and folded into a spiral.

Thomas worked at the table, which doubled as their kitchen, writing longhand in quiet bursts — pausing often to read aloud, revise, or simply look at Eliza, as if to ask: Can we really do this? Her nod, each time, was steady.

They named the manuscript The Last Meriah.

It was not only their love story or a study in ethnography. It was a memory that refused to be erased. A wound that pulsed in the space between conquest and compassion. They wrote with reverence and rage. With tenderness and guilt. Each word felt like a return to the forest — to Shami's stillness, to Amma's hum, to the spirals drawn in ash and turmeric.

They dedicated the book to those "whose voices were not lost, only misheard."

At first, it passed quietly among a few sympathetic scholars. But one day, a professor at King's College hosted a seminar titled "Ritual and Resistance in the Empire's Shadows." A week later, an editorial appeared in The Times Literary Supplement:
"The Spiral Is Not Primitive — It Remembers What Linear History Tries to Forget."

The Last Meriah

Then the letters came.

From a Yoruba linguist in Nigeria: "We too had groves of silence. They were cleared for cotton."
From an Aboriginal elder in Australia: "The loss of our Bora grounds was never acknowledged. Thank you for giving language to that grief."
From a student in Cambridge: "I had never read a love story that made me question my own inheritance."

In libraries and cafés, debates sparked. Young British liberals — especially students and women — began drawing parallels. From the tree-felling in Odisha to rubber plantations in Congo, from Meriah poles to Kenyan sacred fig trees destroyed by colonial roads, the conversations wove themselves into a shared reckoning.

"Were our ancestors only civilizers — or also desecrators?"
"Can knowledge be returned, or only remembered differently?"
"What is it to fall in love across empire — and then listen?"

Even in Parliament, an MP referenced The Last Meriah while proposing an inquiry into colonial forest policy. The book became an anchor text for post-colonial studies. Universities requested talks. Journals ran cover essays. One lecture at the Royal Anthropological Institute was titled:
"The Grove as Archive: Indigenous Knowledge Beyond the Written."

But in the flat, nothing changed. They still shared a kettle, two cups, and one thin quilt. Still argued over grammar and commas. Still kept Amma's seed necklace near the window, where the light fell just right on grey mornings.

The Last Meriah

Some evenings, they would sit without words, listening to distant tram wheels and London's wet hush. Eliza would finger the spiral cloth, and Thomas would reread the page that described their wedding — "no altar, no fire, just breath, dust, and a spiral drawn by barefoot joy."

They never called themselves heroes.
They simply bore witness.
And they wrote what could not be forgotten.

Jitu Mishra

Chapter 39
The Spiral Revisited

"Some stories don't end.
They wait — folded in leaves, carried in
breath, walked back to."

Jitu Mishra

The road was smooth now.

From Phulbani, the car wound through mist-covered hills, past painted school walls, forest outposts, and cell towers. Churches with tin roofs rose beside turmeric drying sheds. Concrete columns stood where once the forest had swallowed paths whole.

Sophie had never been to India.

But in her family, there was a story passed down in fragments. A forest. A woman who listened. A spiral. A love. A return.

Her great-great-grandmother's name was Eliza.
And this land — Kandhamal — had once held her breath.

It wasn't difficult anymore. There were signs now. Maps. An eco-tourism board that welcomed her with brochures about "tribal traditions" and GI-tagged turmeric. The staff offered her tea with hints of ginger and cinnamon. She asked only one thing:

"Is there anyone who remembers the old grove?"

They didn't know.

But an old man at the roadside tea stall paused when he heard the question. His name was Lakshman Majhi, his face folded with time. He turned to the woman beside him — his wife, Dasi, who was wrapping turmeric bulbs in banana leaves — and said,

"You mean the British woman who wore no boots? The one who married under a tree?"

Jitu Mishra

Sophie blinked. "You know about her?"

The couple nodded, slow and sure.

They took her walking — down a trail not marked on any brochure. The air was heavy with rain-quiet. The earth smelled of roots.

"It was here," Dasi whispered, pointing to a ring of sal trees, "where they tied the cloth."

The grove had changed. The sacred pole was gone, but someone had planted turmeric in a spiral. In the center, a single sal sapling rose tall.

"They stayed two seasons," Lakshman said.
"We were children. But our Amma remembered. She said the woman cried when she left. Not for sadness. For being held."

Sophie knelt and touched the earth.

"It's still warm," she said.

Later, at the Sunday market, she saw the turmeric stalls — piles of golden rhizomes wrapped in jute and straw, labeled with shiny tags:
"Kandhamal Haldi – GI Certified. Aromatic. Ancestral."

Buyers came from Bhubaneswar, Mumbai, Delhi.

But beneath the scent, Sophie sensed something else — rituals still remembered in the way the roots were washed, how women placed leaves clockwise in bowls, how elders still told children: "Don't step across the spiral when it's drawn."

Jitu Mishra

She opened her notebook. She didn't write.
She just drew — a faint spiral.

That evening, Lakshman brought out a small cloth parcel. Inside was a dried bark panel. Faint, but still visible — a spiral etched with charcoal and ash.

"My grandfather said it was left by a woman who never tried to speak our language, but listened better than most who did."

Sophie held it to her chest, the forest dimming into the folds of dusk.

She did not ask what happened to Eliza and Thomas.
She didn't need to.

They had walked the spiral.
And now, she had returned.

Chapter 40
A Spiral for the Future

"What was once sacred is now necessary.
What was once dismissed may yet save
us."

The Last Meriah

When Sophie returned to London, it was late autumn.
The city was wrapped in greys and sirens.
But her palms still smelled of turmeric, and her mind
hummed with the hush of sal leaves.

She unpacked slowly.

The bark panel was wrapped in mulberry paper. The
spiral on it had faded slightly, but she traced it every
morning — not to remember Kandhamal, but to remain
within it.

She didn't know immediately what she would do with all
she had gathered. But slowly, it became clear.

Not a memoir.
Not a field report.
Something else.

A reckoning.
A translation.
A spiral for the world that had lost its ground.

The film began with silence.
A camera panning slowly across the forest floor of
Kandhamal.
The bark.
The turmeric.
The spiral drawn by a child's foot.

No narrator. Just breath and birds.

Then came the voices.

Jitu Mishra

The Last Meriah

Lakshman and Dasi, remembering.
A schoolteacher talking about how Meriah songs were being woven into children's lessons.
A turmeric farmer explaining soil care not by pH levels, but by reading the way worms curved in the loam.

Later came echoes from elsewhere:
A Kichwa woman from Ecuador speaking of medicinal vines.
A Sámi elder describing how snow speaks if you still know how to listen.
A Maasai farmer explaining rotational grazing without ever using the word "science."

And Sophie?
She didn't appear until the last frame.
Not to explain.
Just to sit — beside a spiral drawn in turmeric dust, book in one hand, earth in the other.

The film was called:
"Roots That Remember: Indigenous Wisdom in a Dying World."

Within months, it was screened at COP.
Then at the Royal Society.
Then at a climate gathering in Geneva where no one applauded at the end. They just sat still, breathing like forest.

An editorial in The Guardian read:

"The film does what policy papers fail to: it listens."
Another in Le Monde:
"It is not about the past. It is about what we forgot we still need."

Jitu Mishra

The Last Meriah

Sophie didn't call herself an activist.
Nor an anthropologist.
When asked who she was, she would simply say,

"A woman who walked a spiral drawn before she was born."

And on her desk — beneath maps and notebooks and film stills — sat The Last Meriah.
Worn.
Underlined.
Tattooed by time.

Next to it, the bark spiral.
Still faint.
Still alive.

And every now and then, when the wind rattled the window just right, she would close her eyes and hear the grove.

"Some stories are not concluded.
They are planted.
And what they grow into —
is not ours to own,
only to water."

Jitu Mishra

Epilogue
The Spiral I Walked

For the longest time, I wrote the story to completion. Only during the writing did I realise the story was also writing me. Perhaps history is not finished. Perhaps the spiral has room yet for everyone willing to turn and listen. For in a world turned blind with urgency, to reclaim memory is itself an act of resistance. And in the soil of Kondh rites, I found the seeds of another world: one that might listen before it takes, one that would let the turmeric bloom. And so I leave the spiral at your feer. Rooted, and repeating. Stepping out. Ready to be walked again.

—Jitu Mishra

The Last Meriah

Jitu Mishra is a storyteller and archaeologist whose novels explore the intersections of landscape, memory, and cultural exchange. Known for Pepper and Tides and Whispers of the Tea Leaves, he now turns inward with The Last Meriah — a lyrical journey into ritual, resilience, and the wisdom of silence.
He lives in Bhubaneswar, listening to stories the land still keeps.

When Eliza arrives in 19th-century Kandhamal, she believes she is here to document a dying custom. Instead, she becomes part of a living resistance — one carried not by swords, but by spirals of turmeric and memory. As the Meriah sacrifice fades, the forest begins to speak — of kinship, courage, and the quiet power of remembering.

Over a century later, her descendant Sophie walks the same red soil. Amid roads, markets, and schools, she discovers echoes of a ritual that never truly ended. What began as an anthropological inquiry becomes a global reckoning — linking Kandhamal to Amazonia, Kenya to Australia, and memory to survival.

The Last Meriah is a novel about the love that listens, the rituals that endure, and the forests that teach us how to live again.